The Clever Wife: A Kyrgyz Folktale
Text © Rukhsana Khan 2022
Illustrations © Ayesha Gamiet 2022

Wisdom Tales in an imprint of World Wisdom, Inc.

Library of Congress Cataloging-in-Publication Data

Names: Khan, Rukhsana, 1962- author. | Gamiet, Ayesha, illustrator.
Title: The clever wife : a Kyrgyz folktale / told by Rukhsana Khan ;
illustrated by Ayesha Gamiet.
Description: Bloomington, Indiana : Wisdom Tales, 2022. | Audience: Ages
4-8. | Audience: Grades 2-3. | Summary: A young maiden named Danyshman
draws the attention and admiration of the ruling Khan Bolotbek, but will
he forgive his clever wife when she breaks her promise to him?
Identifiers: LCCN 2021037429 (print) | LCCN 2021037430 (ebook) | ISBN
9781937786939 (hardback) | ISBN 9781937786946 (epub)
Subjects: CYAC: Folklore--Kyrgyzstan.
Classification: LCC PZ8.1.K5523 Cl 2022 (print) | LCC PZ8.1.K5523 (ebook)
| DDC 398.2/095843 [E]--dc23
LC record available at https://lccn.loc.gov/2021037429
LC ebook record available at https://lccn.loc.gov/2021037430

Printed in China on acid-free paper.

For information address Wisdom Tales,
P.O. Box 2682, Bloomington, Indiana, 47402-2682
www.wisdomtalespress.com

The Clever Wife

A Kyrgyz Folktale

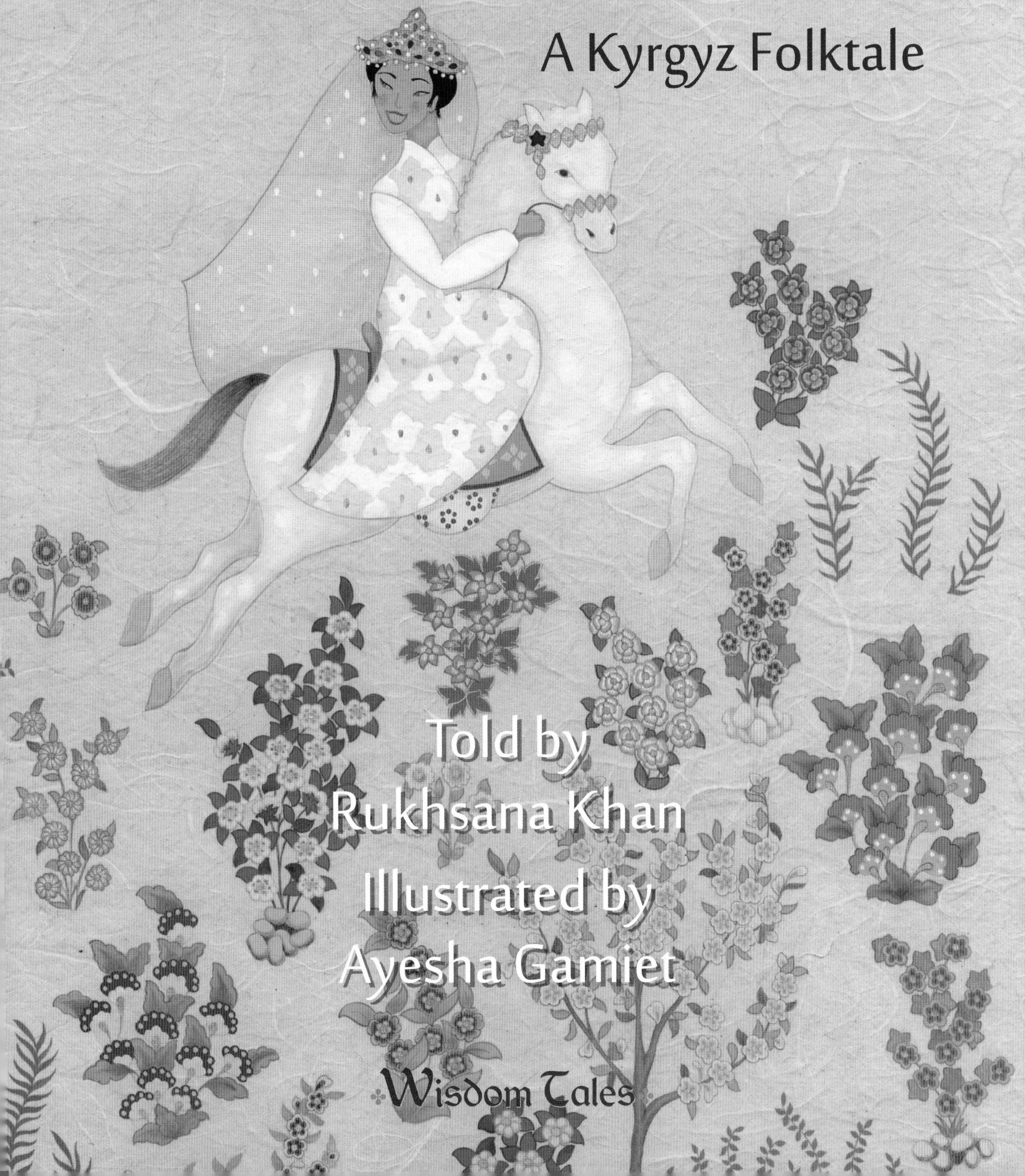

Told by
Rukhsana Khan
Illustrated by
Ayesha Gamiet

Wisdom Tales

When the old khan Sarybay felt the end of his life was near, he gathered his people and told them to choose their next leader.

The people said, "You are wise. Appoint a new khan and we shall honor him."

"Very well, I have a faithful white falcon. When I die, set him free. He will land on the shoulder of your next khan."

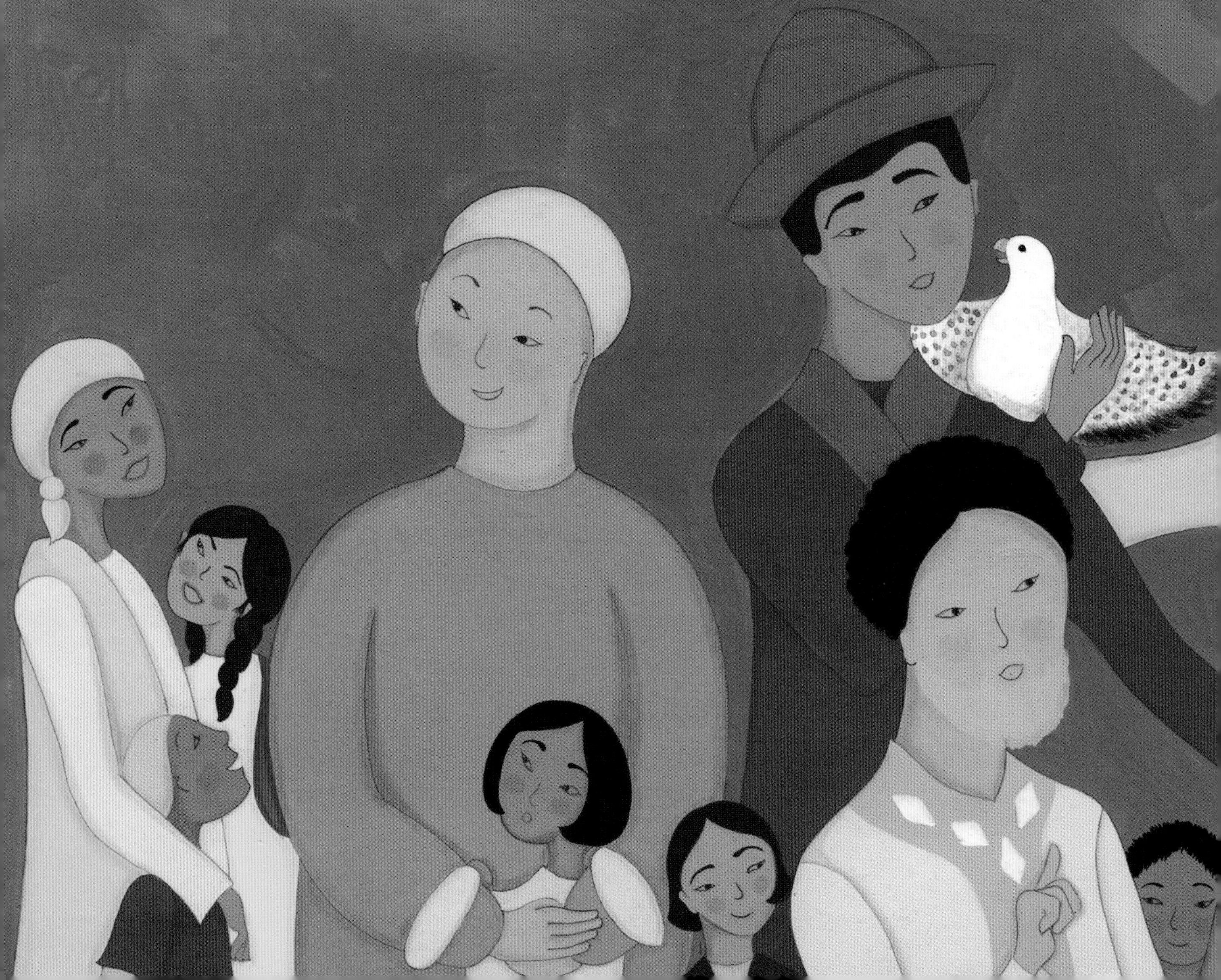

When Sarybay died, a crowd gathered. The falcon circled the air three times and landed on a youth named Bolotbek.

Some shouted, "He is too young."

Others cried, "Shall we bow to a shepherd boy?"

But the elders said, "Remember Sarybay. Give him a chance."

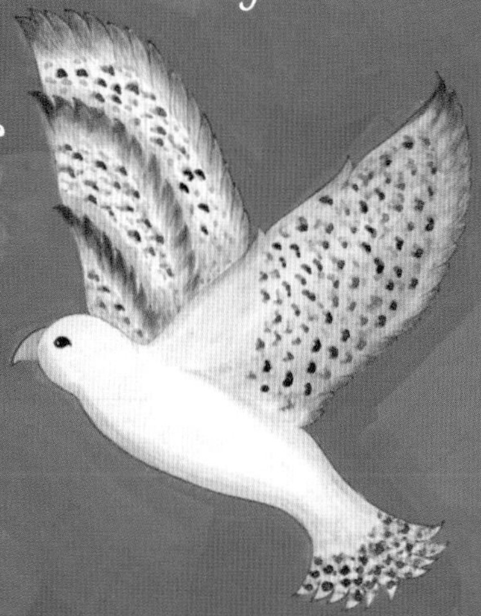

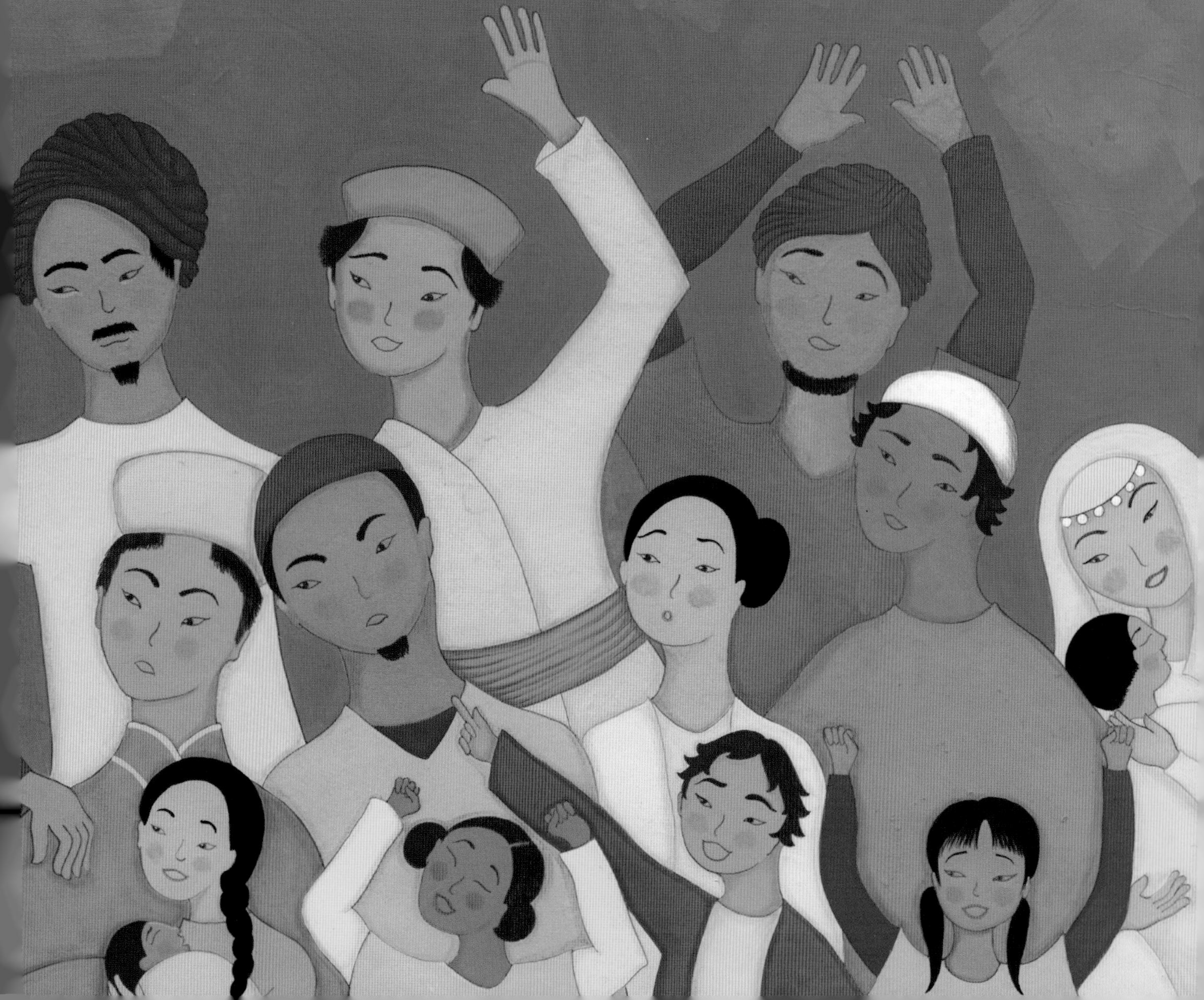

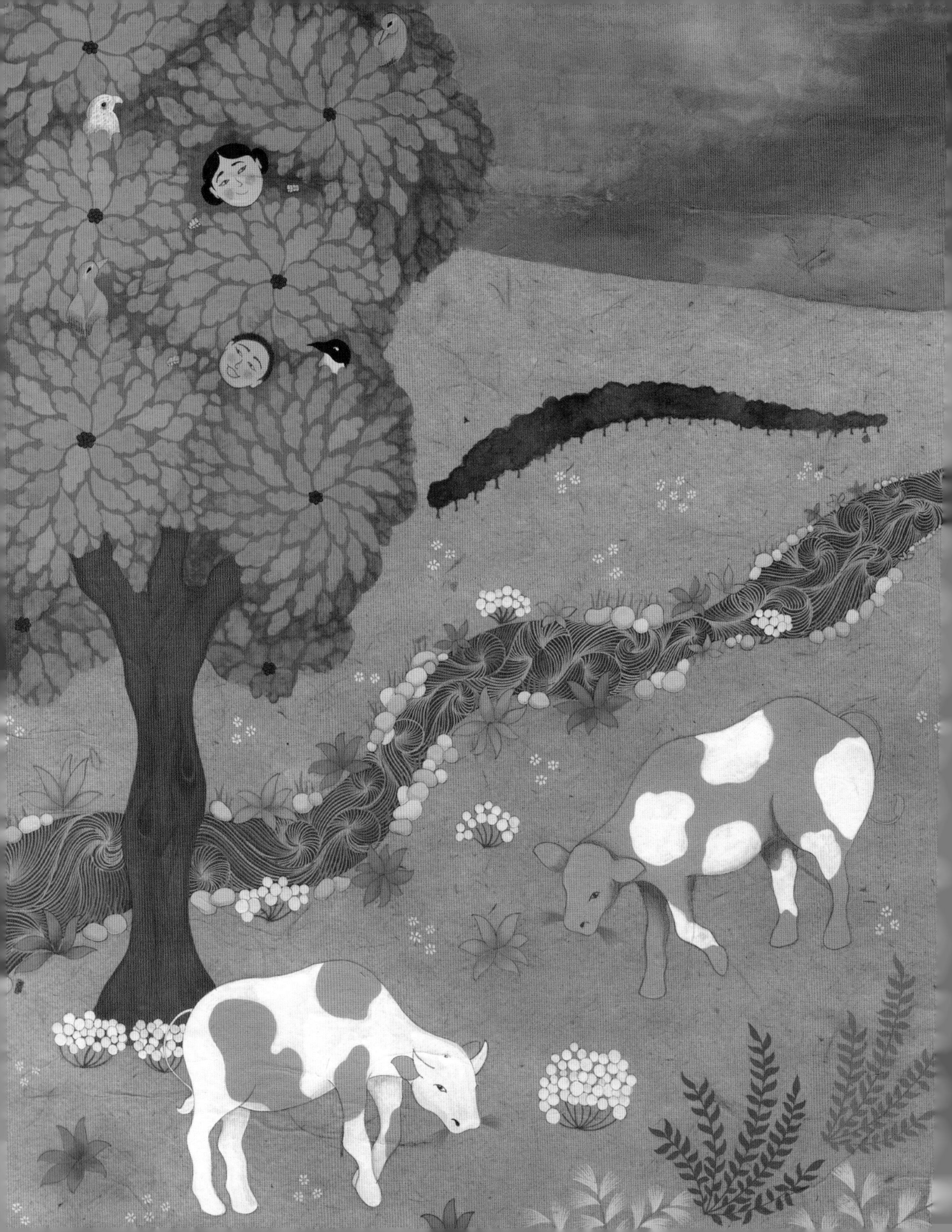

And so the shepherd Bolotbek became the khan of the land. He ruled with justice. He provided for the poor from his own storehouses.

Soon, his subjects grew to revere him.

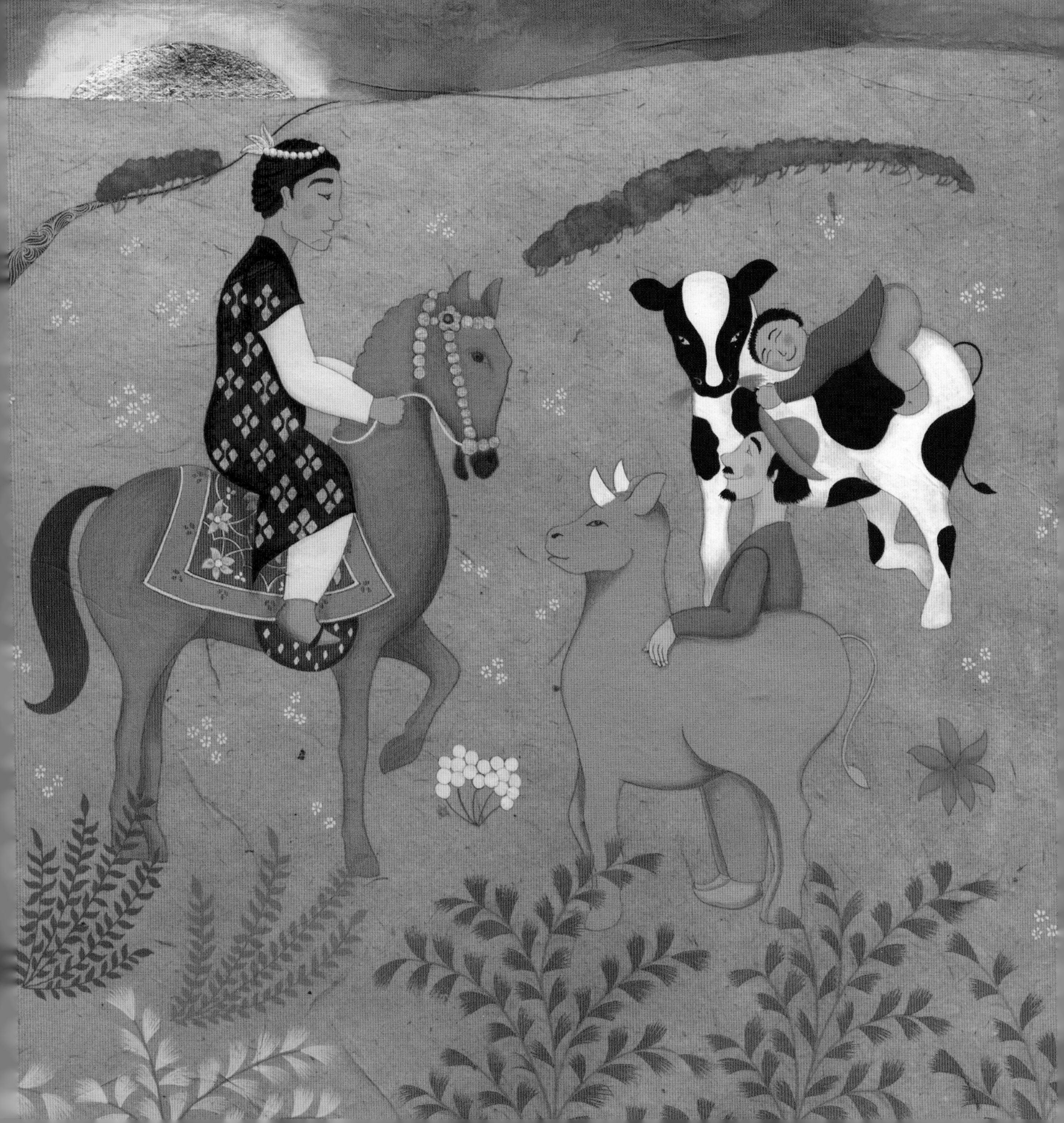

But as time passed the people worried that Bolotbek did not take a wife. The elders begged him to marry so that he would have an heir to continue to rule peacefully.

Bolotbek said, "Fine, gather the maidens of the khanate. I will ask them three riddles. Whoever gives me the best answer will be my wife."

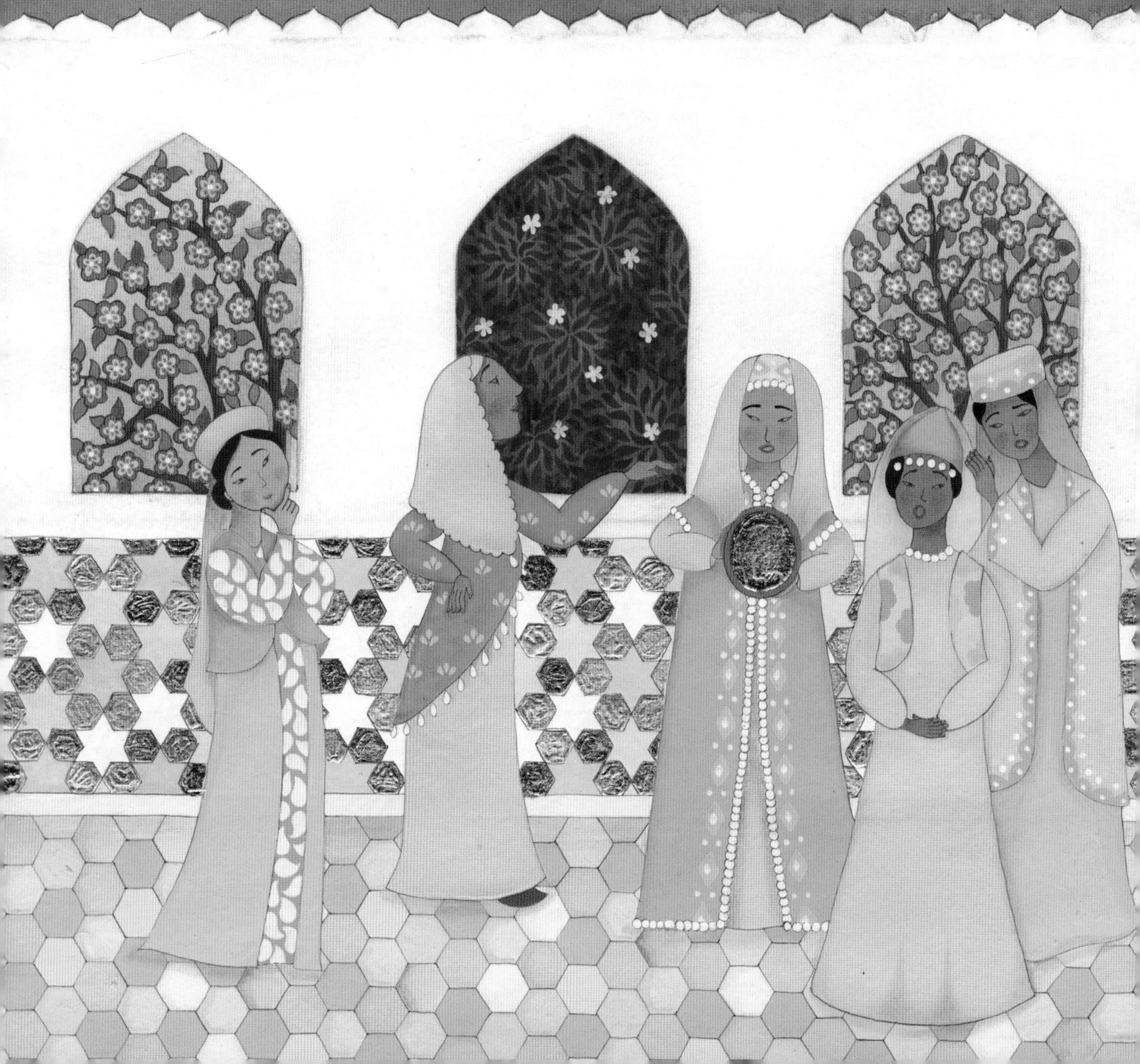

Many high born maidens gathered.

Bolotbek asked, "What is the distance between the east and the west? What is the distance between the earth and the sky? What is the distance between truth and falsehood?"

For two days the maidens tried to answer.

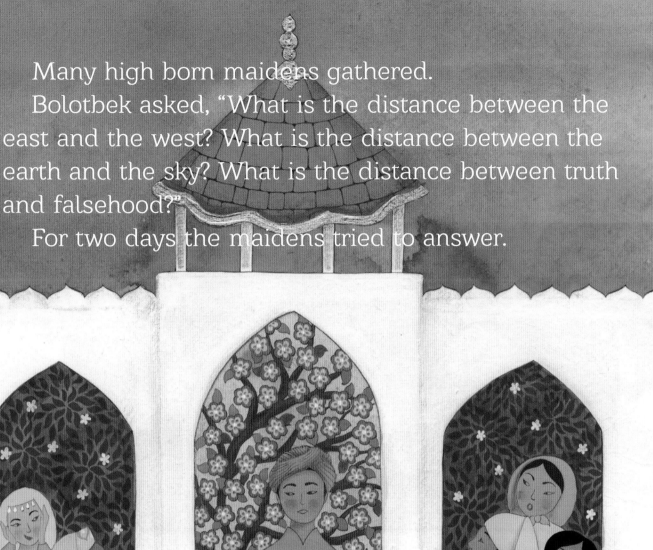

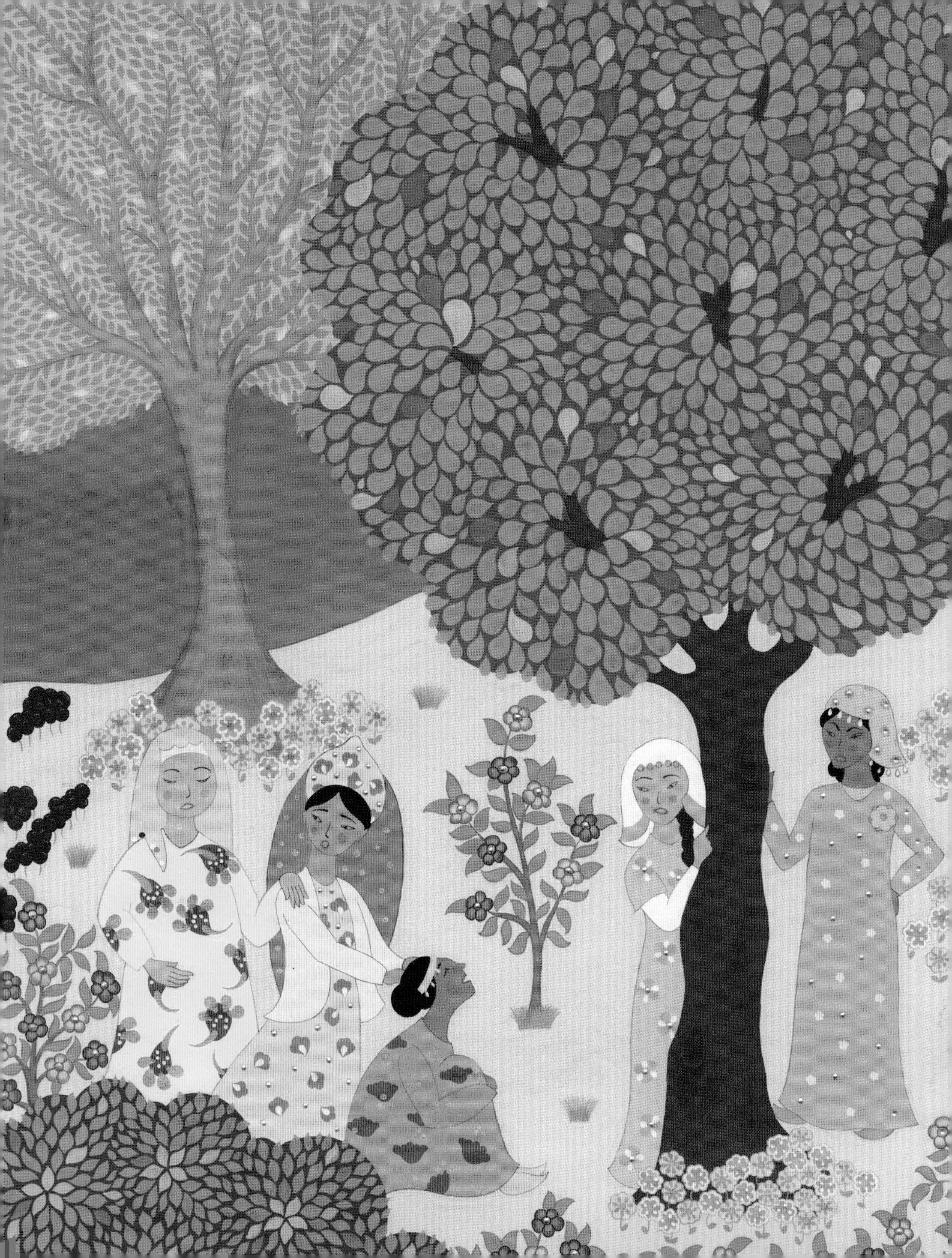

As they approached the palace on the third day, they met a poor girl named Danyshman.

She said, "Sisters, why do you go back and forth to the palace?"

Some of the maidens said, "It's none of your affair!" But one of them was kind and told her. Danyshman begged to go with them. Some mocked her, but the kind one allowed her to come.

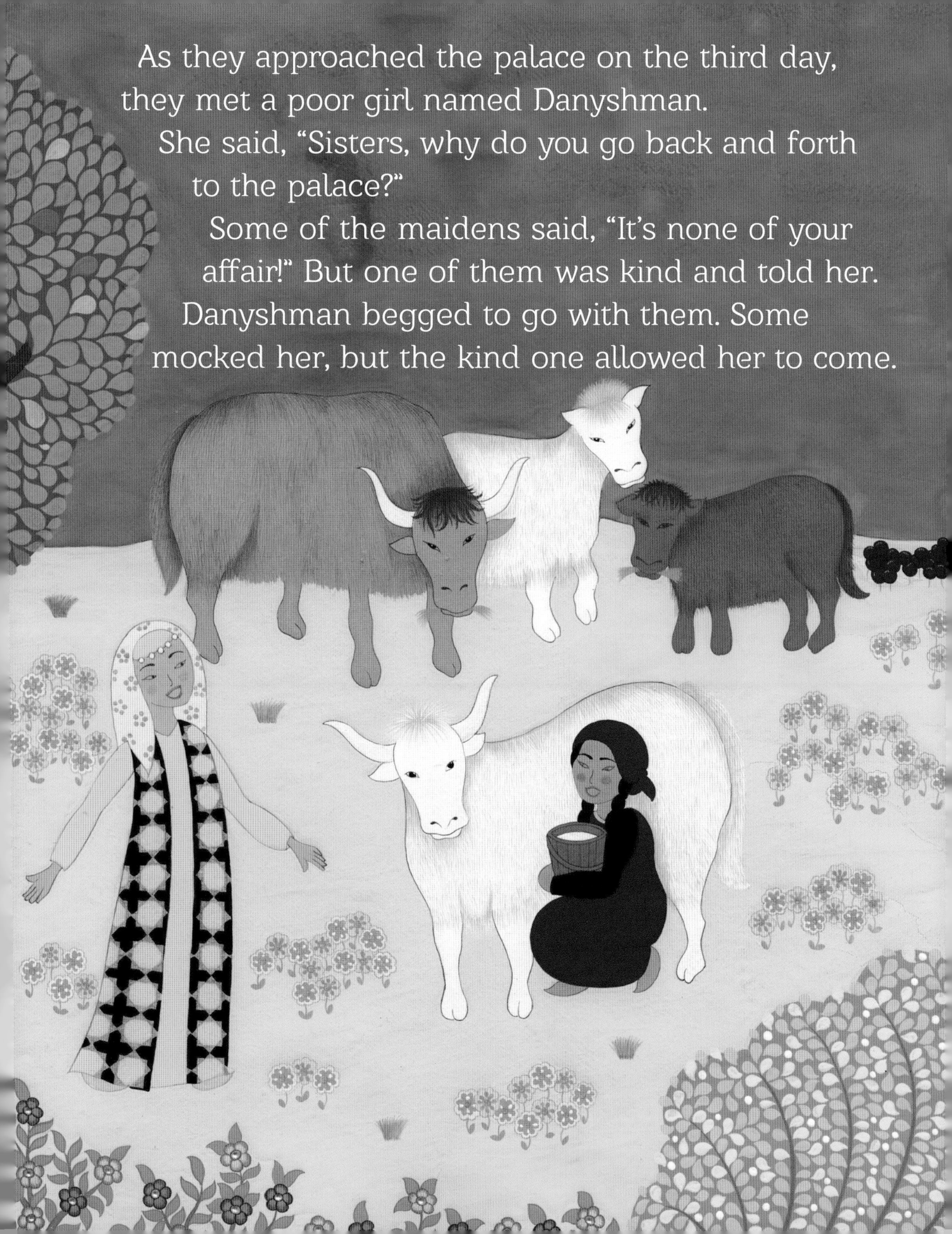

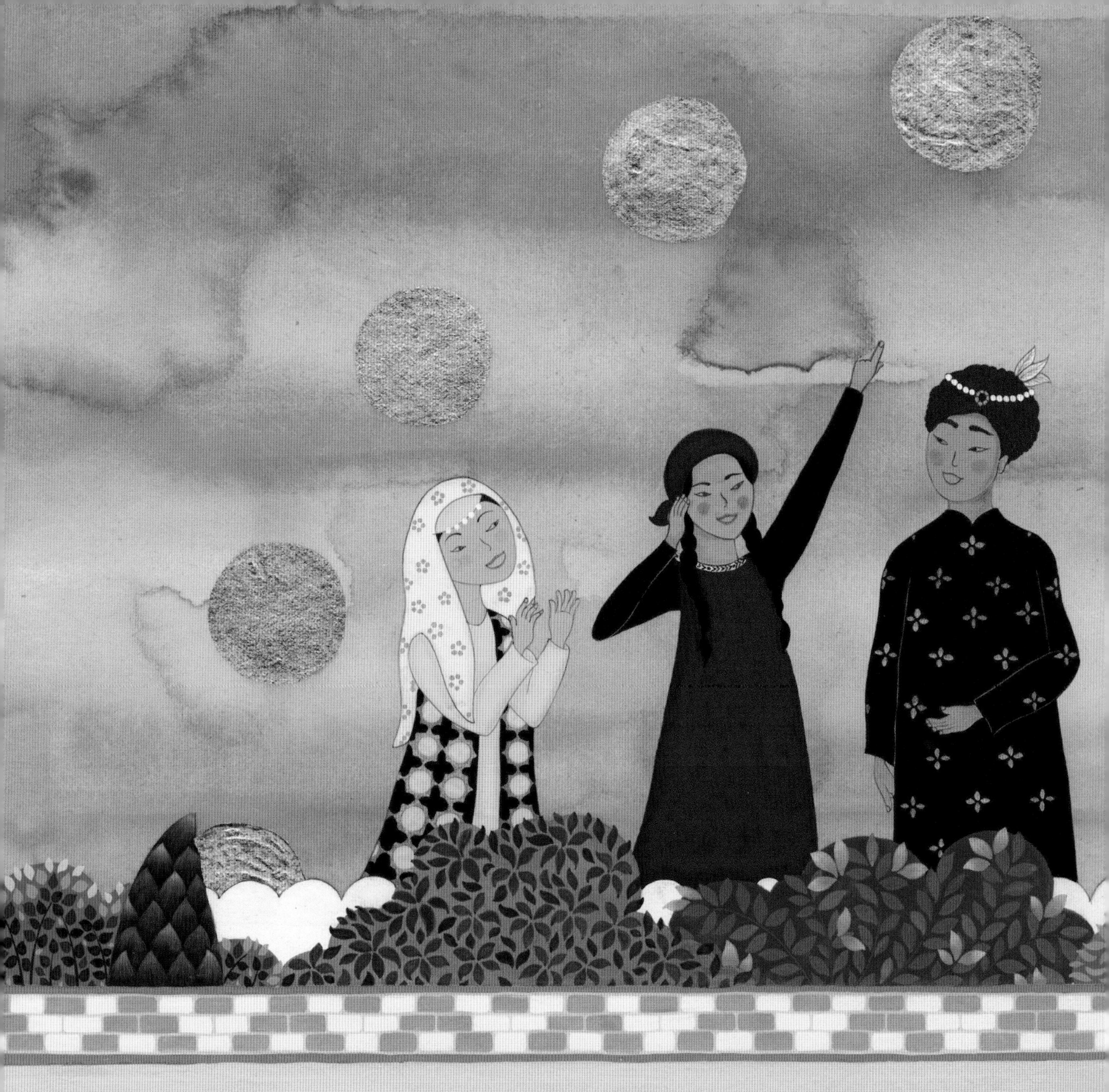

At the palace, Bolotbek said, "Well? Who can answer?"

Danyshman stepped forward. "The distance between the east and west is one day's journey, for in the morning the sun starts in the east and ends in the west in one day's time. The distance between the earth and sky is easily encompassed by the eye, for the eye looks

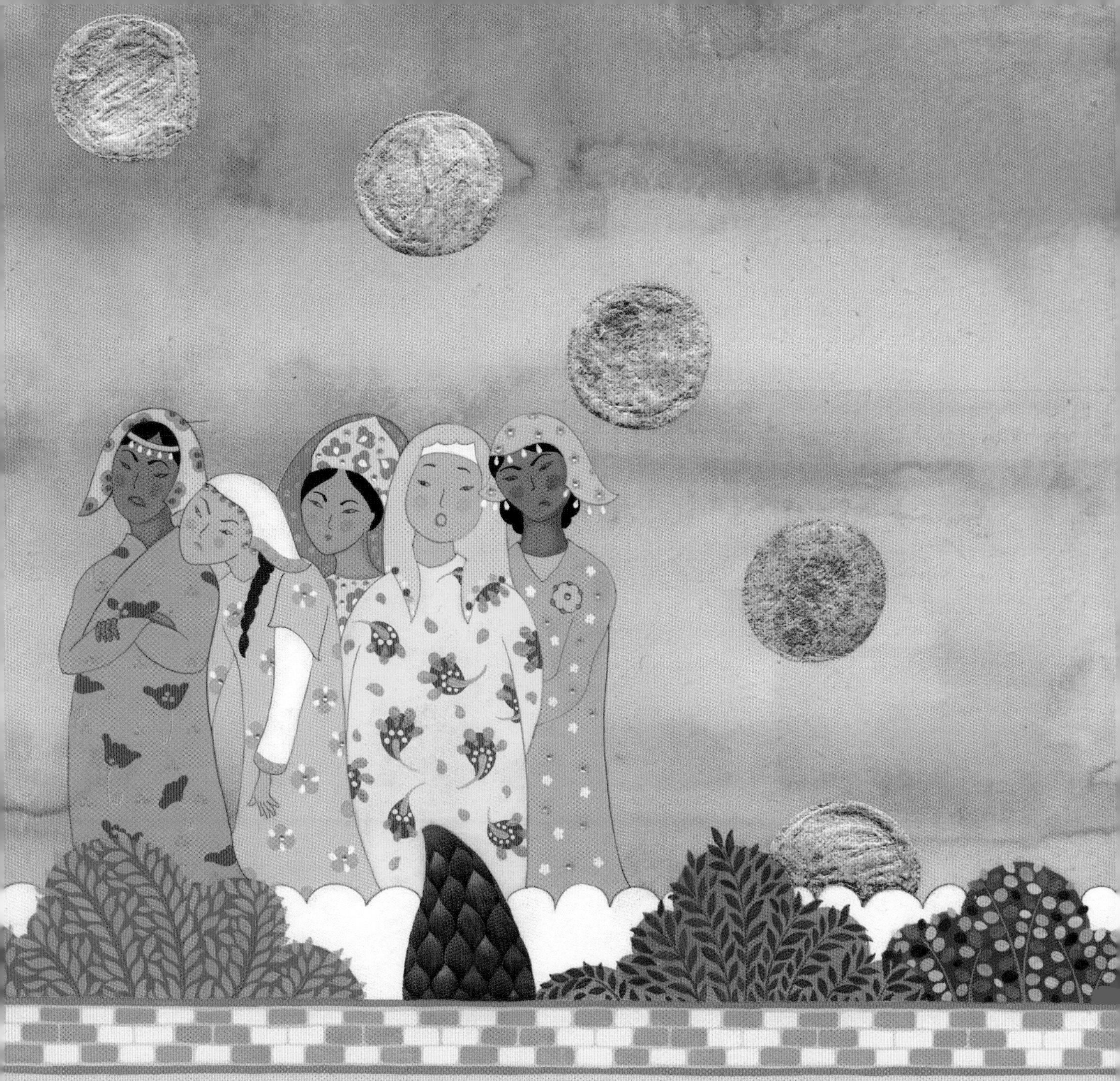

down and sees the earth, then looks up and sees the sky. The distance between truth and falsehood is the width of four fingers: it is the distance between the ear and eye, for the ear hears the falsehood but the eye sees the truth."

Bolotbek said, "You are wise. I will marry you!"

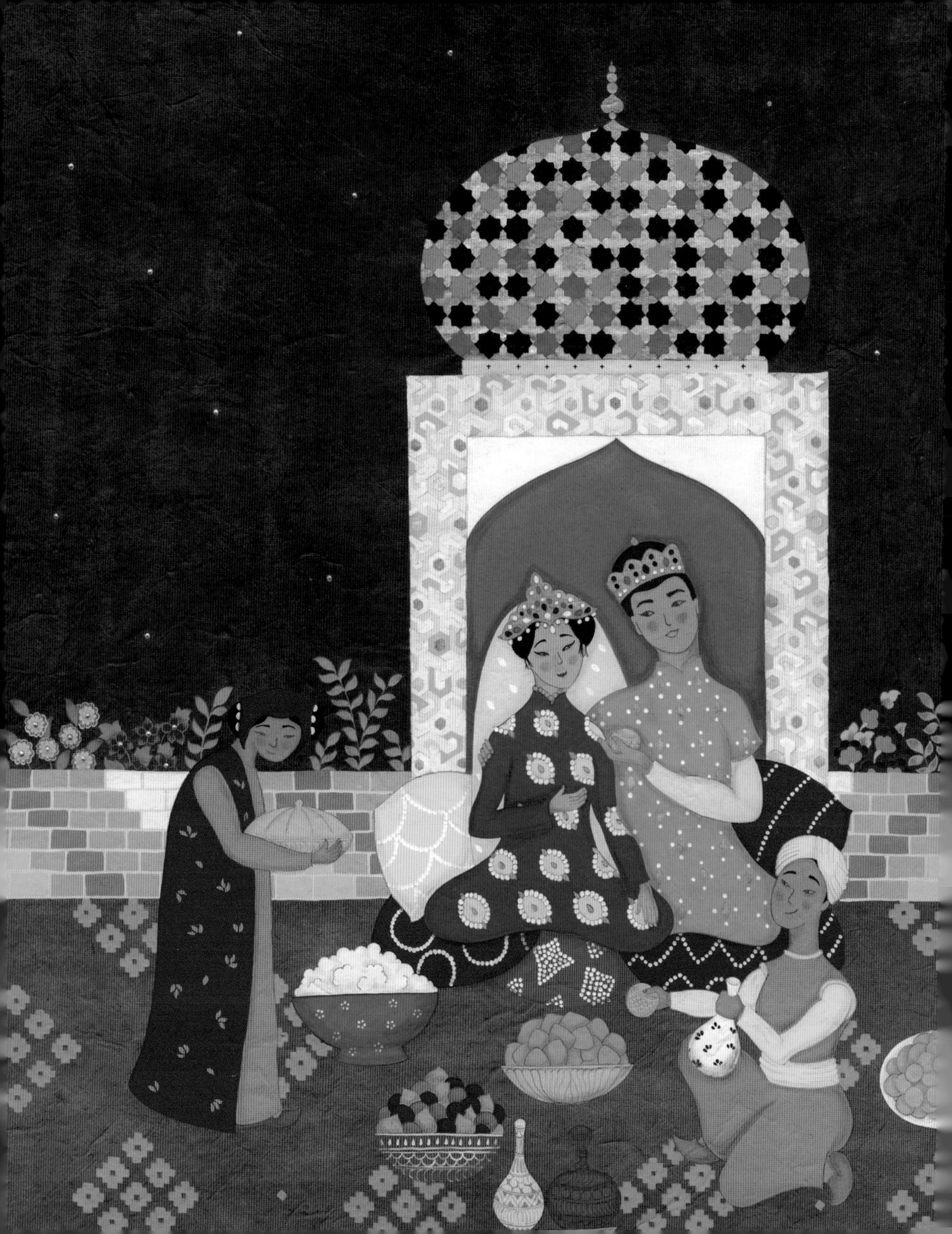

That night Bolotbek told Danyshman, "I think we will be very happy together. But I want you to promise me one thing."

"What's that?"

"I don't want you to share your wisdom with any other person, only me."

Danyshman promised.

The two lived happily together. Both remembered their days of poverty and did all they could to help the poor.

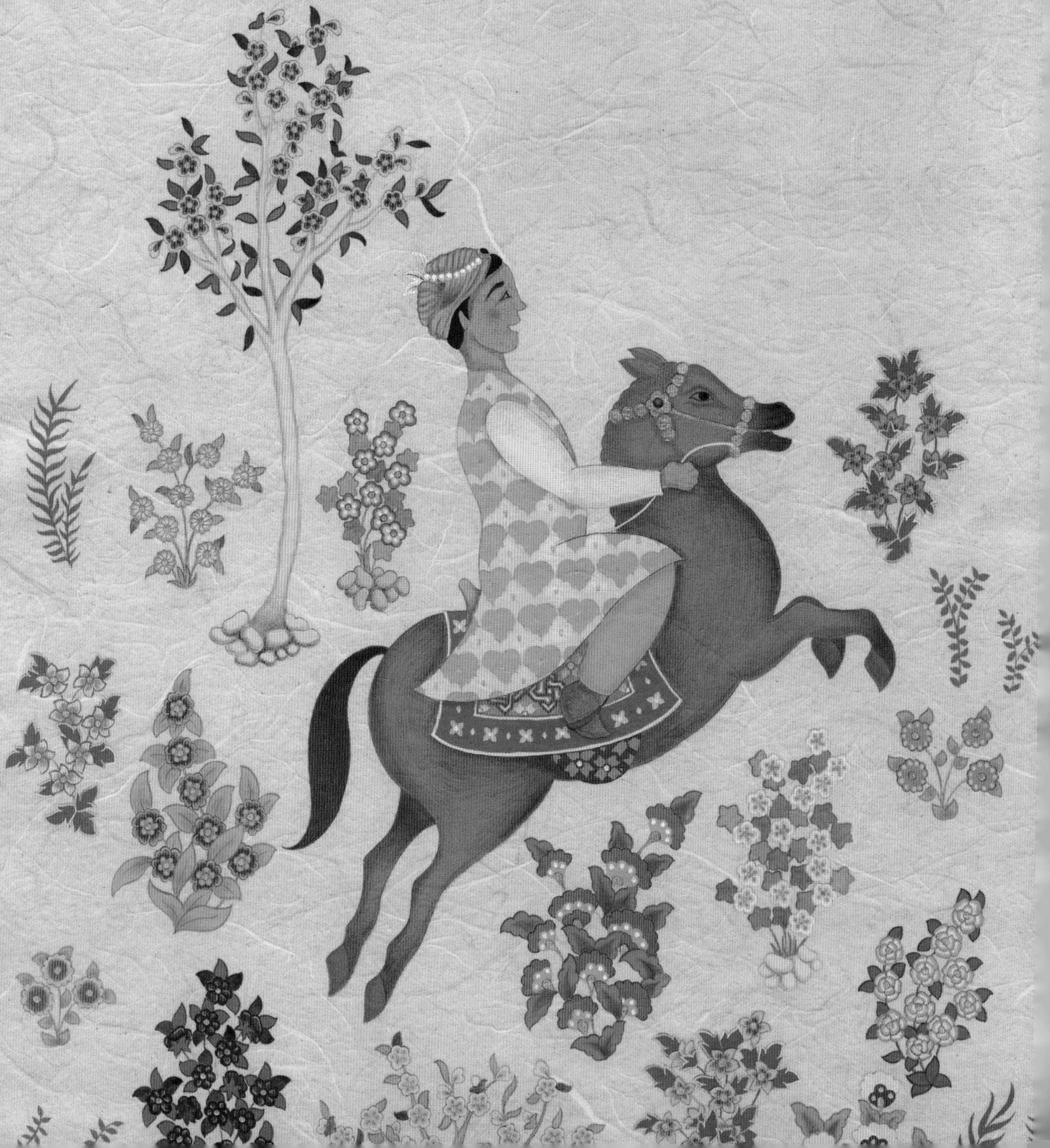

Whenever Bolotbek had a difficult decision, he consulted wise Danyshman for advice. And so they both ruled with justice.

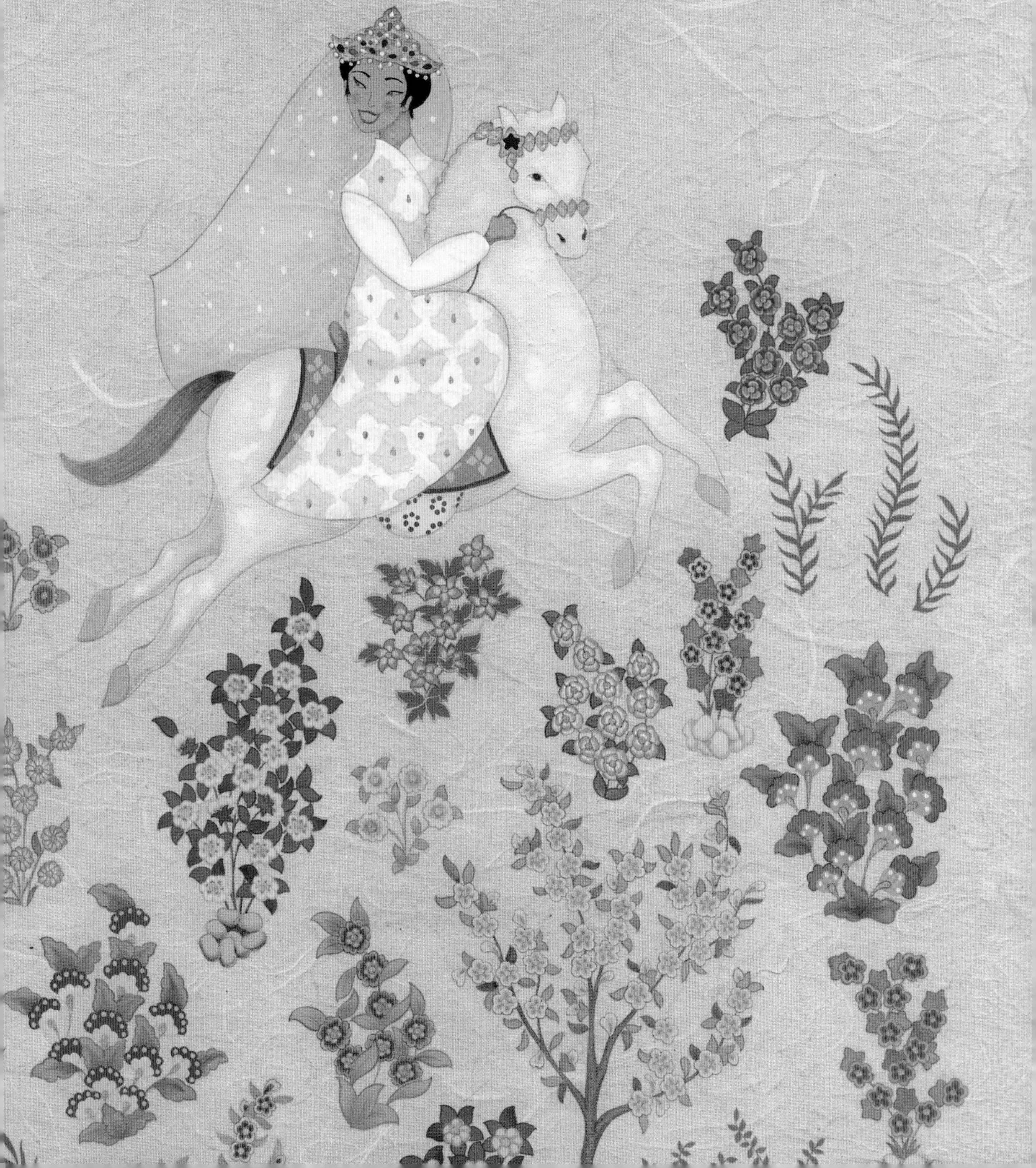

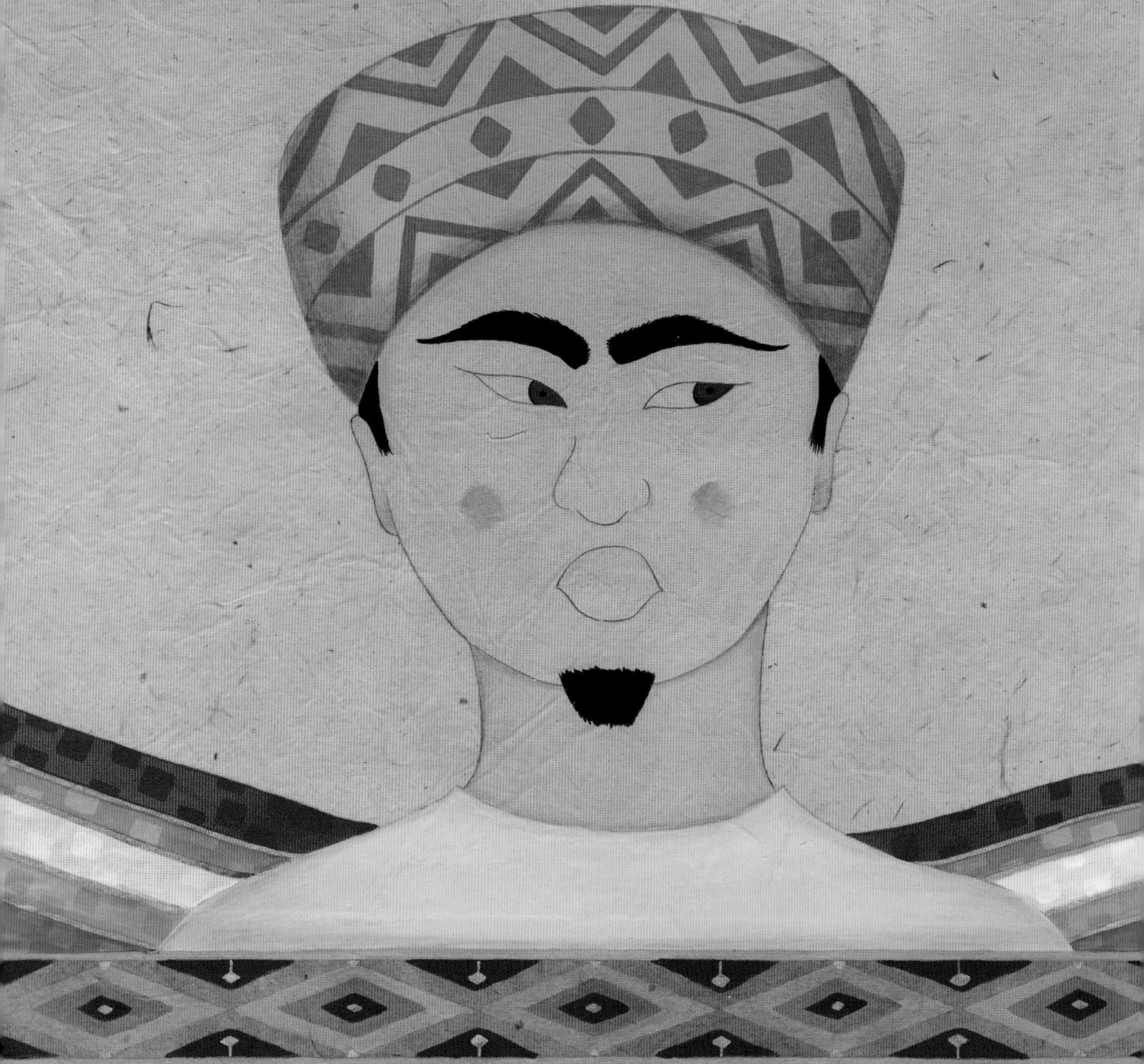

But one day a man committed a crime for which the punishment was death.

He would face Bolotbek to be judged.

He begged Danyshman to tell him what to say to avert the punishment.

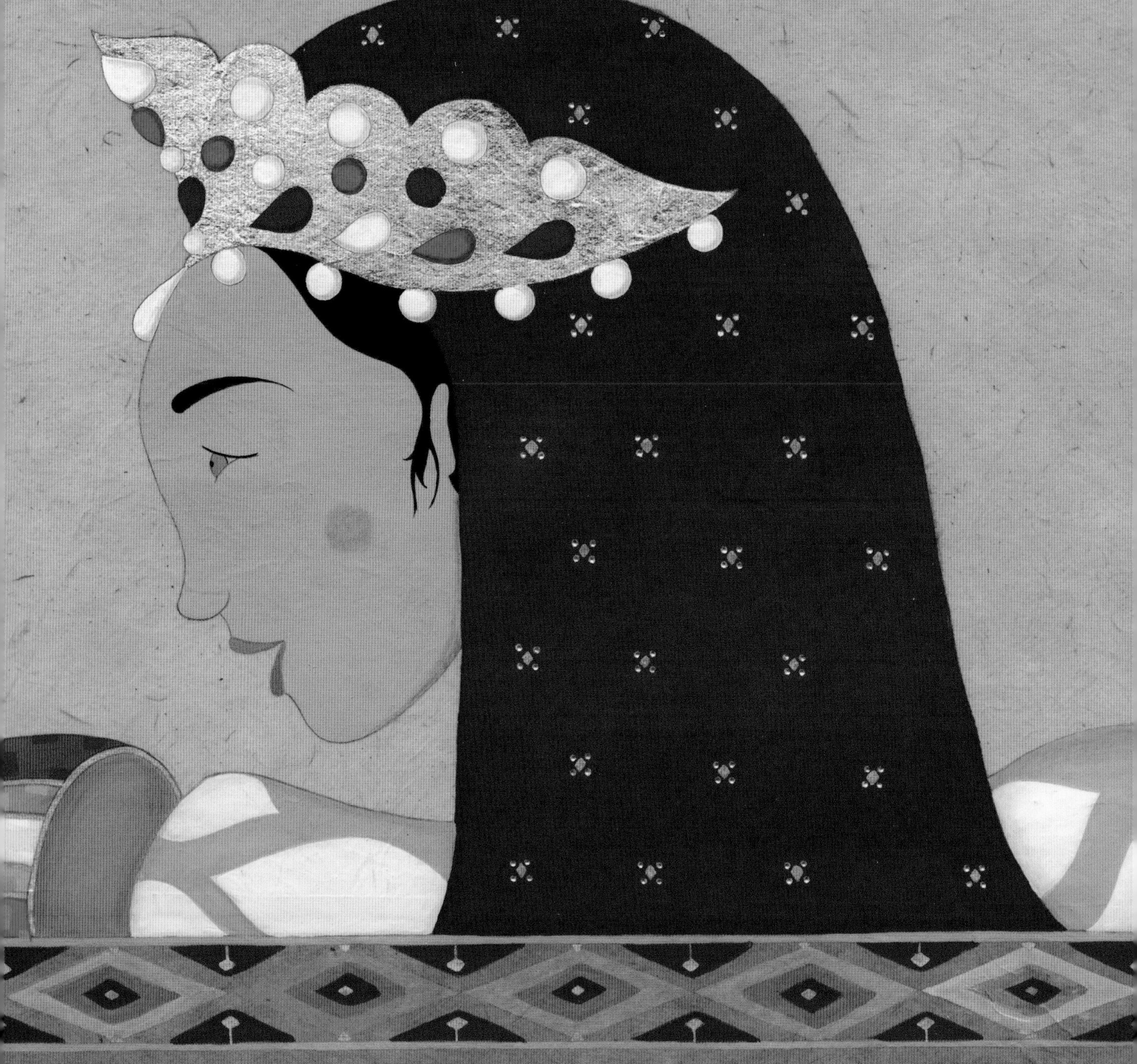

Danyshman said, "I cannot tell you."
"But I'm going to die!"
So Danyshman told him what to say, but asked him not to tell Bolotbek or she would be in great trouble. The man promised.

When the man was presented with the charges, he gave such an ingenious answer that Bolotbek could not apply the punishment of death. Bolotbek grew suspicious. The man did not look clever enough to have thought of such a response.

Bolotbek said, "Who told you to say such a thing?"

"I cannot tell you."

Bolotbek said, "Tell me or I will apply the punishment anyway!"

The man said, "It was Queen Danyshman!"

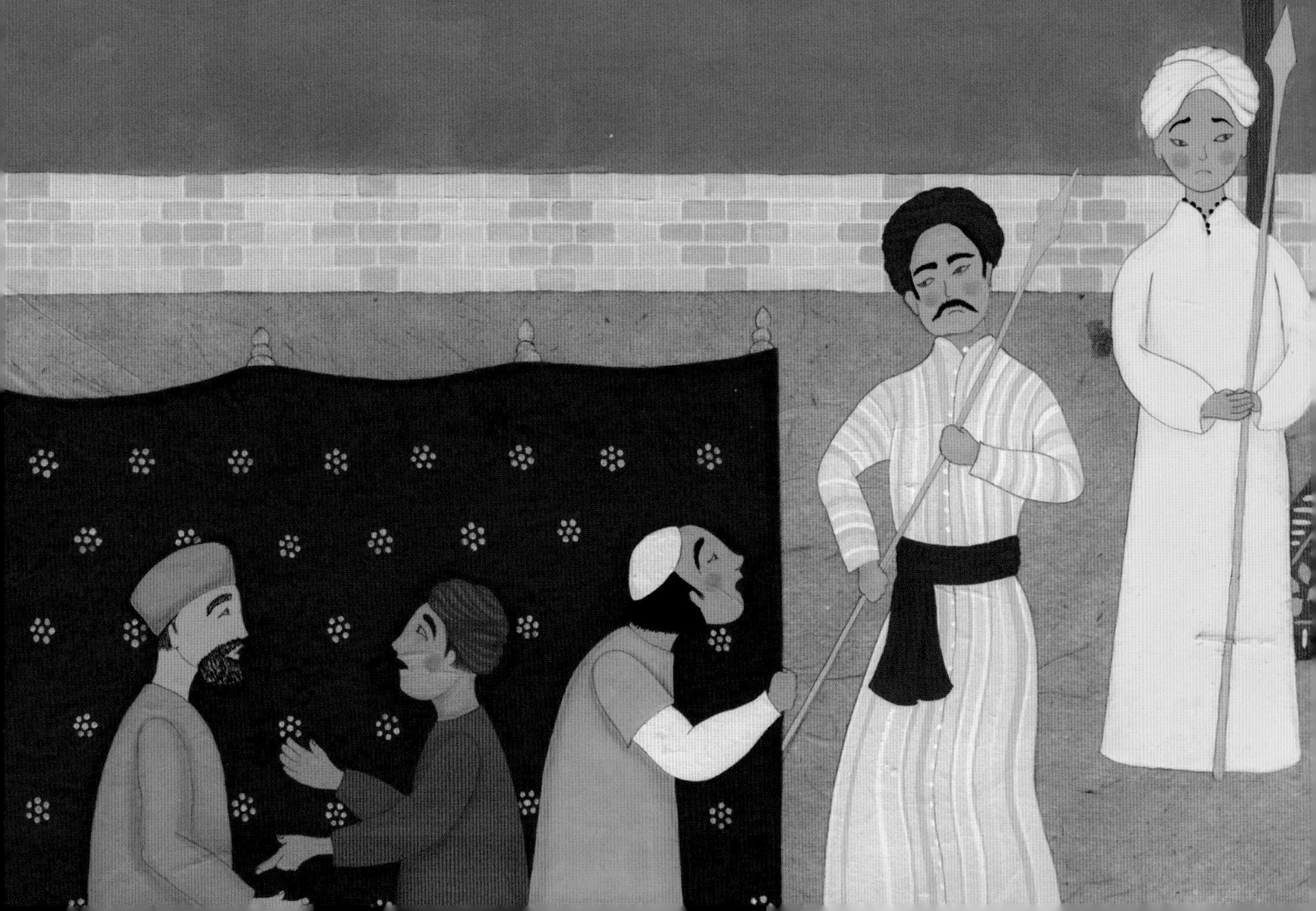

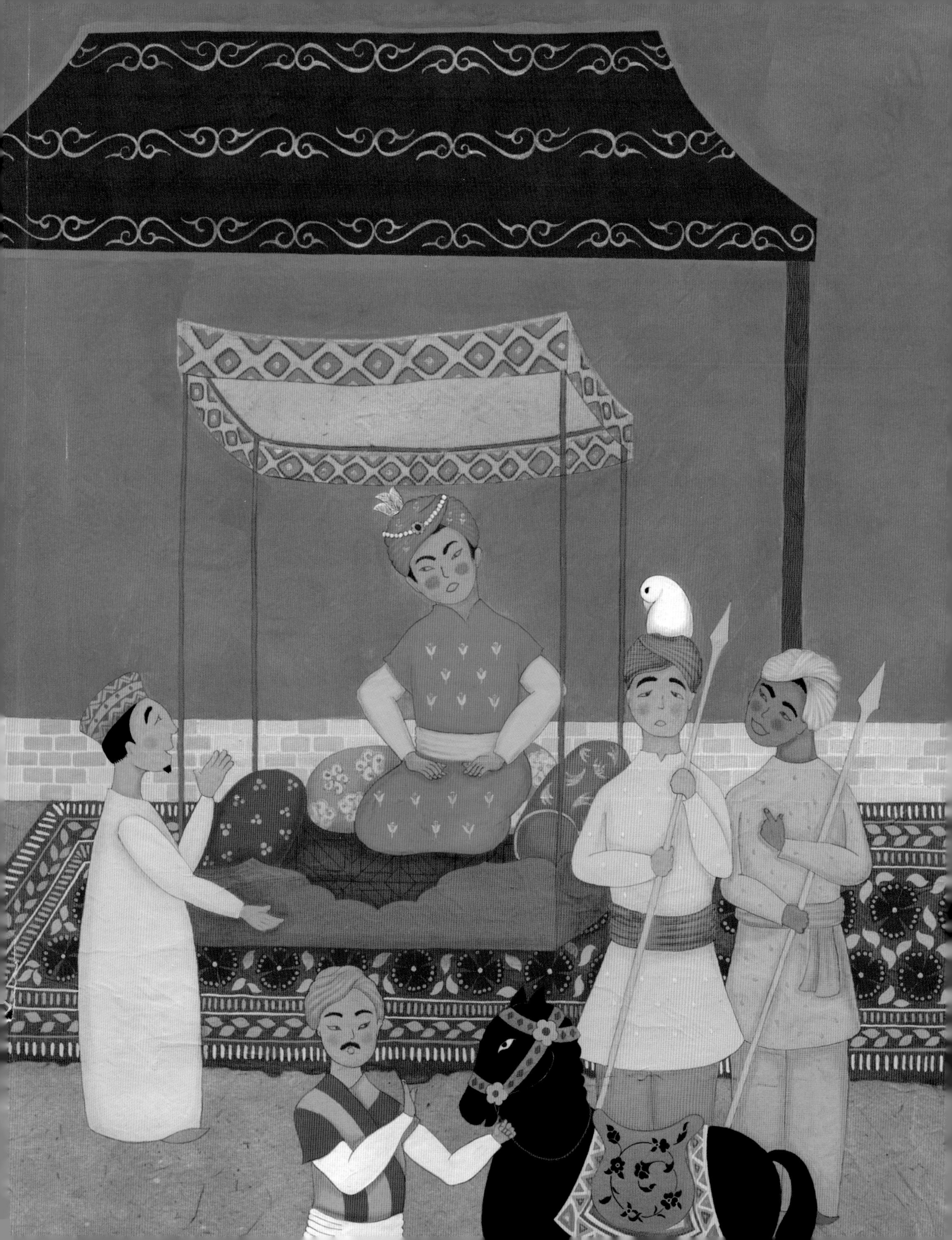

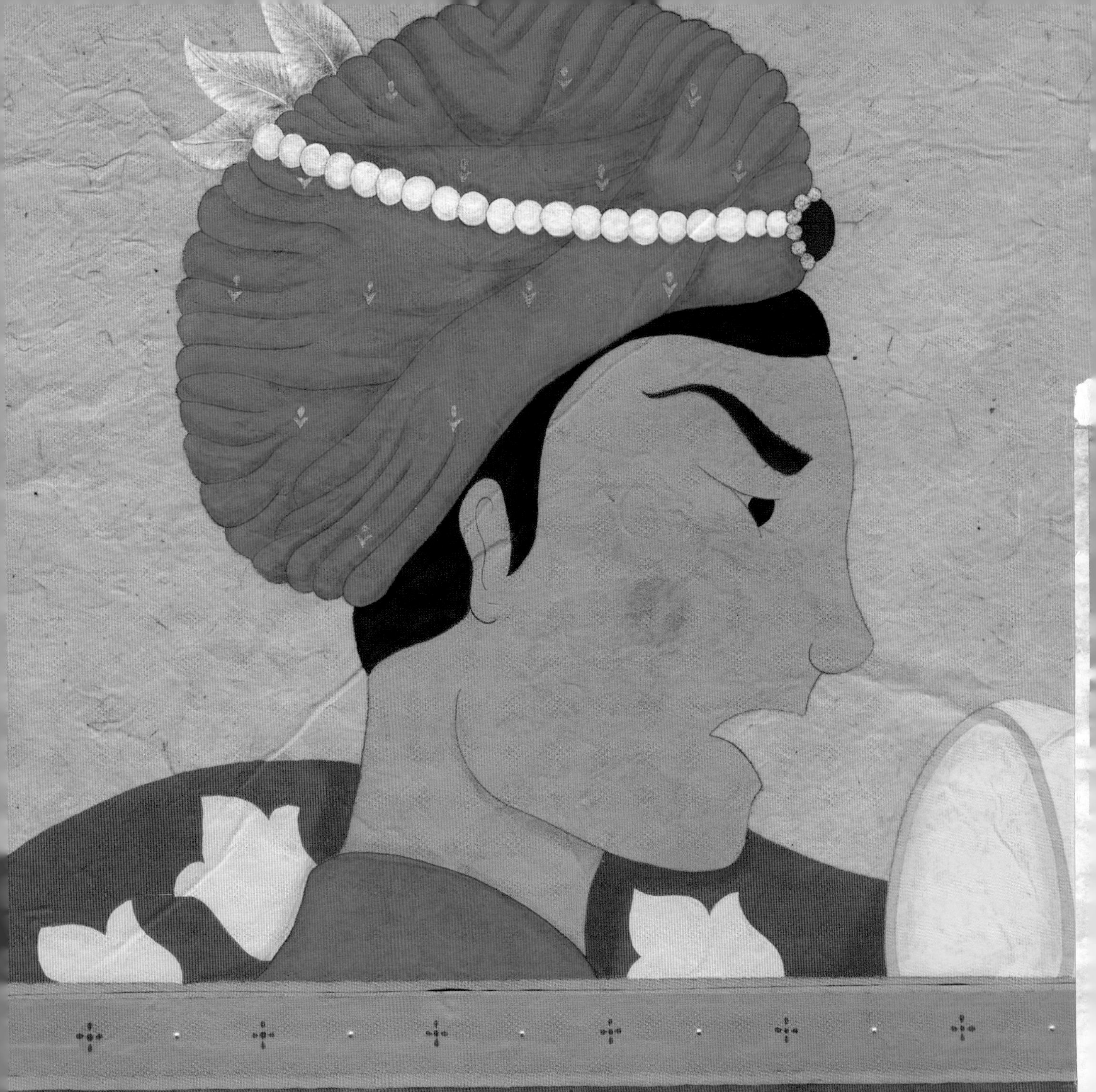

Bolotbek stormed into his chambers. "Danyshman, you have betrayed me! You promised you would not share your wisdom with anyone else, but you have shared it with another man!"

"Yes," said Danyshman.

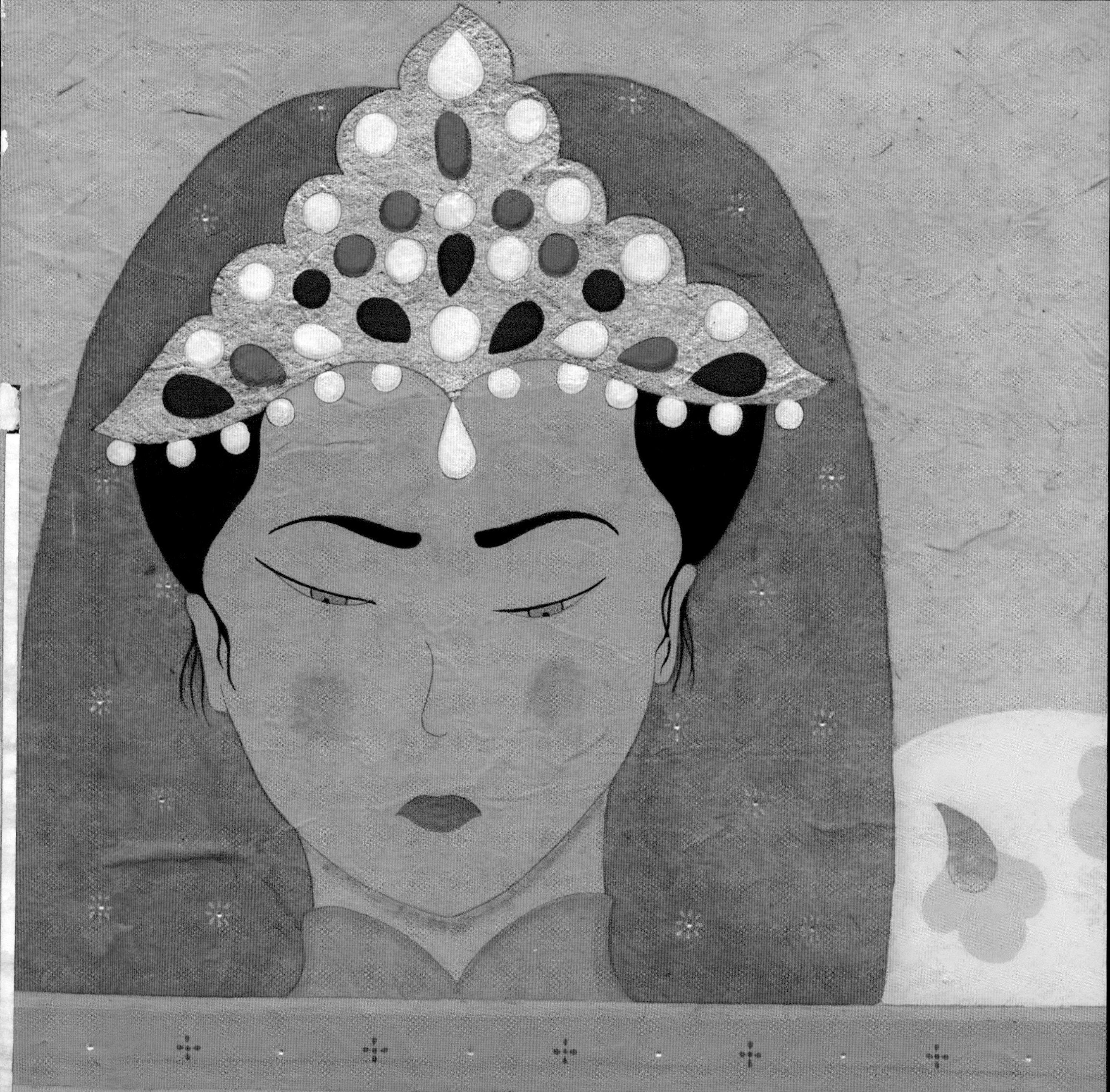

"You must go! Take whatever is most precious to you and leave my khanate."

"Very well," said Danyshman. "But before I go, would you dine with me one last time?"

Bolotbek agreed.

Danyshman prepared all his favorite meals and set them on a long table in the garden. She nibbled slowly as they reminisced about the good times they'd had together.

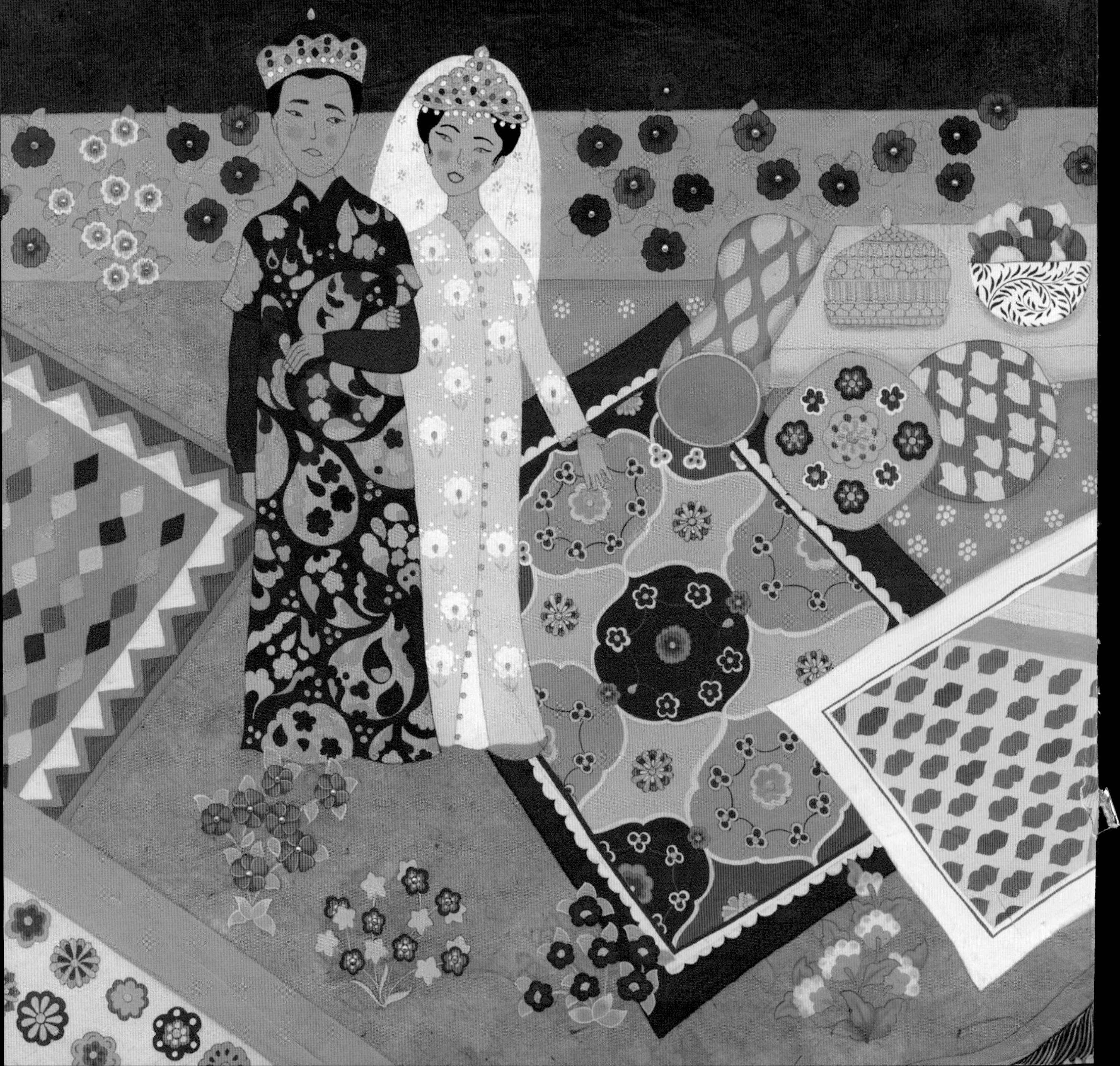

When she got tired, she strolled around the garden. Bolotbek joined her.

Then she returned to the table and nibbled a bit more, making the meal last a very long time.

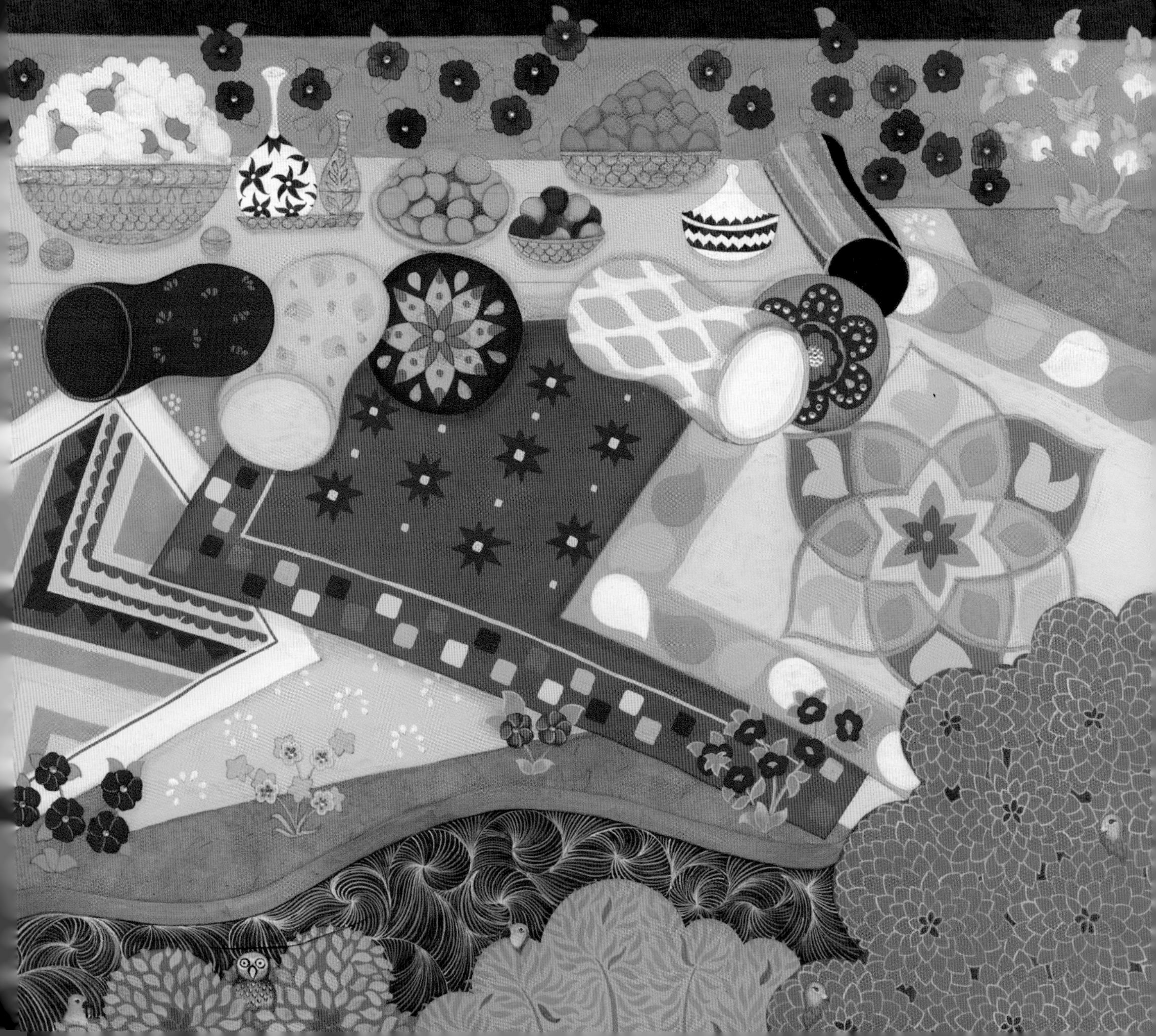

Bolotbek grew drowsy from the rich food.

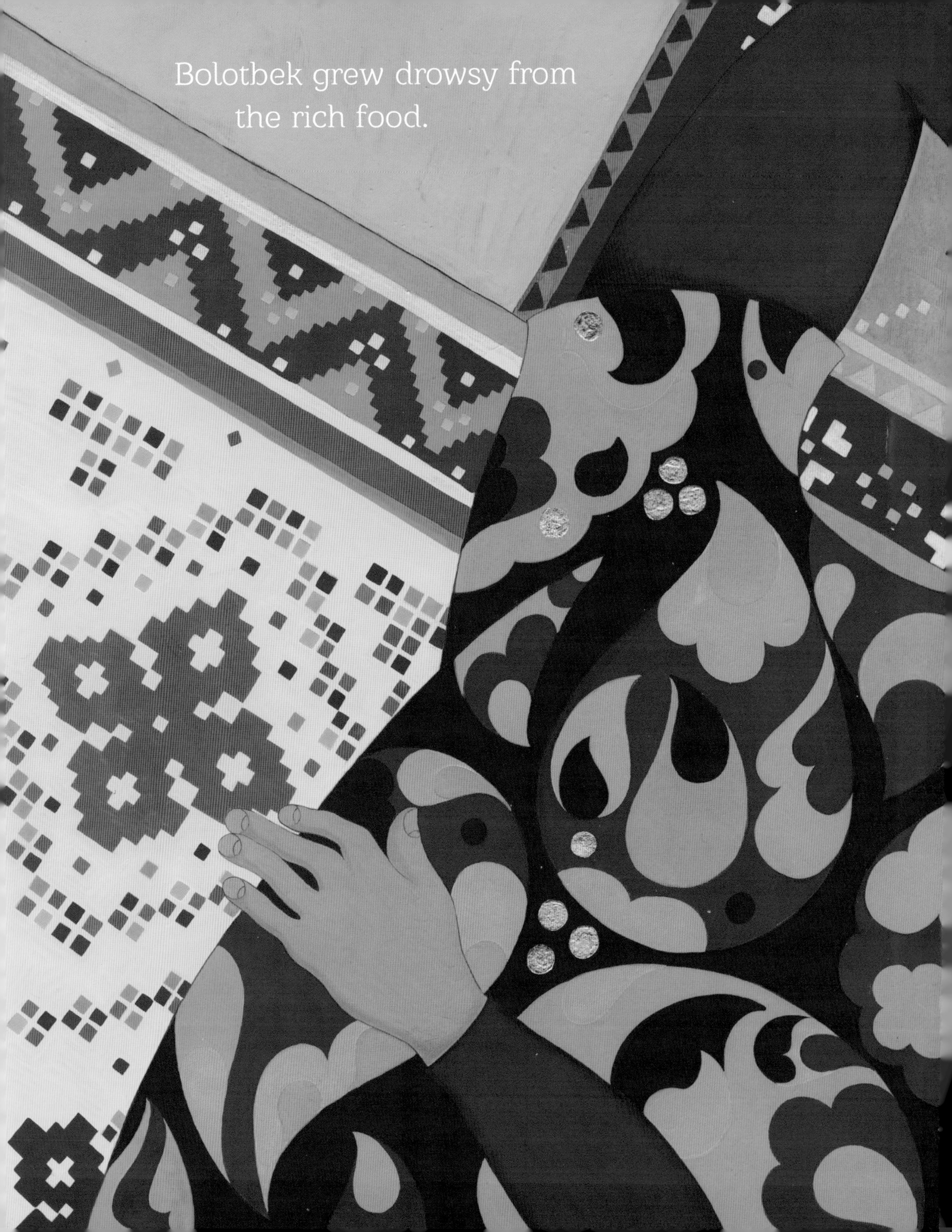

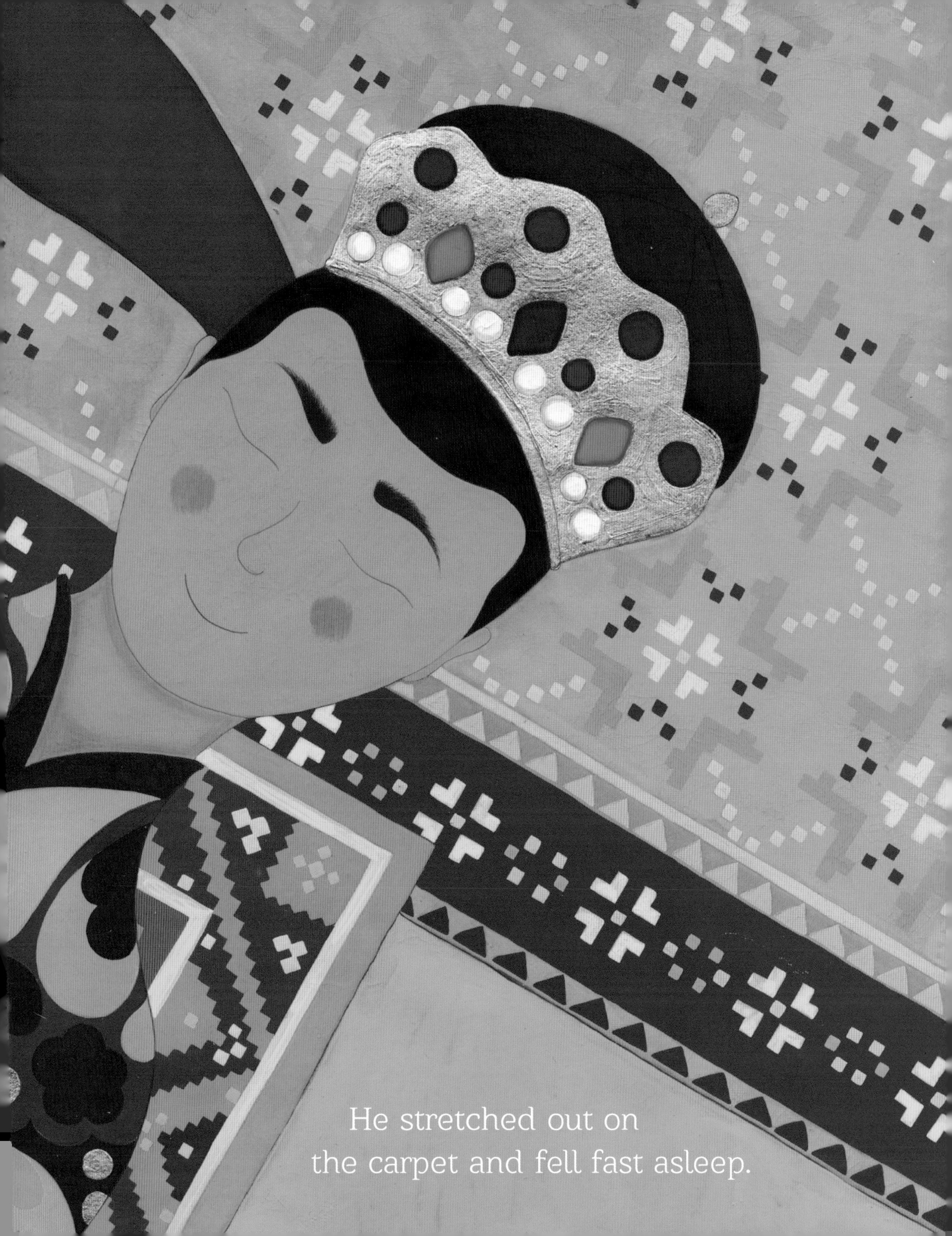

He stretched out on
the carpet and fell fast asleep.

Danyshman rolled him up and had the servants load the carpet onto a cart.

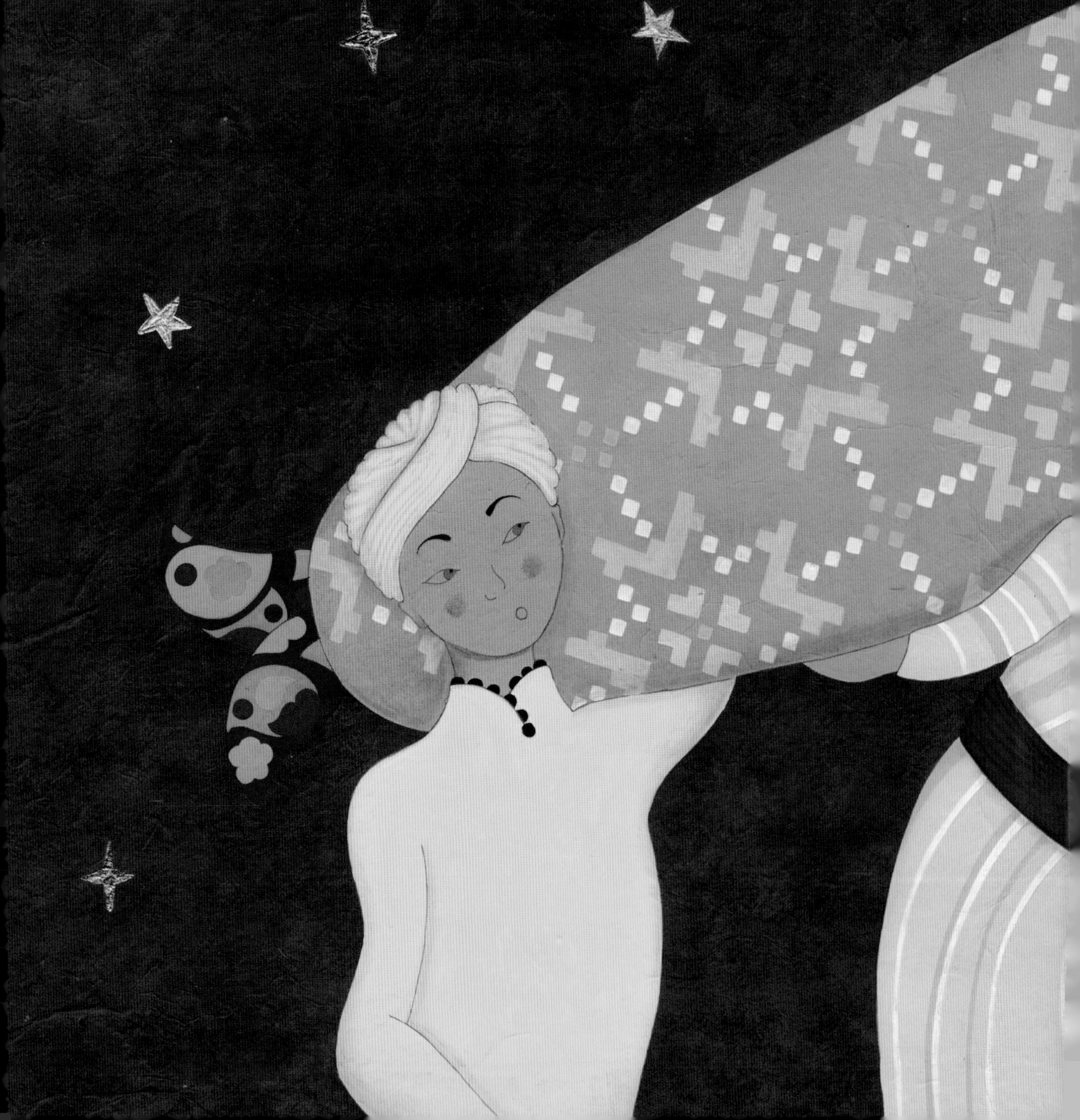

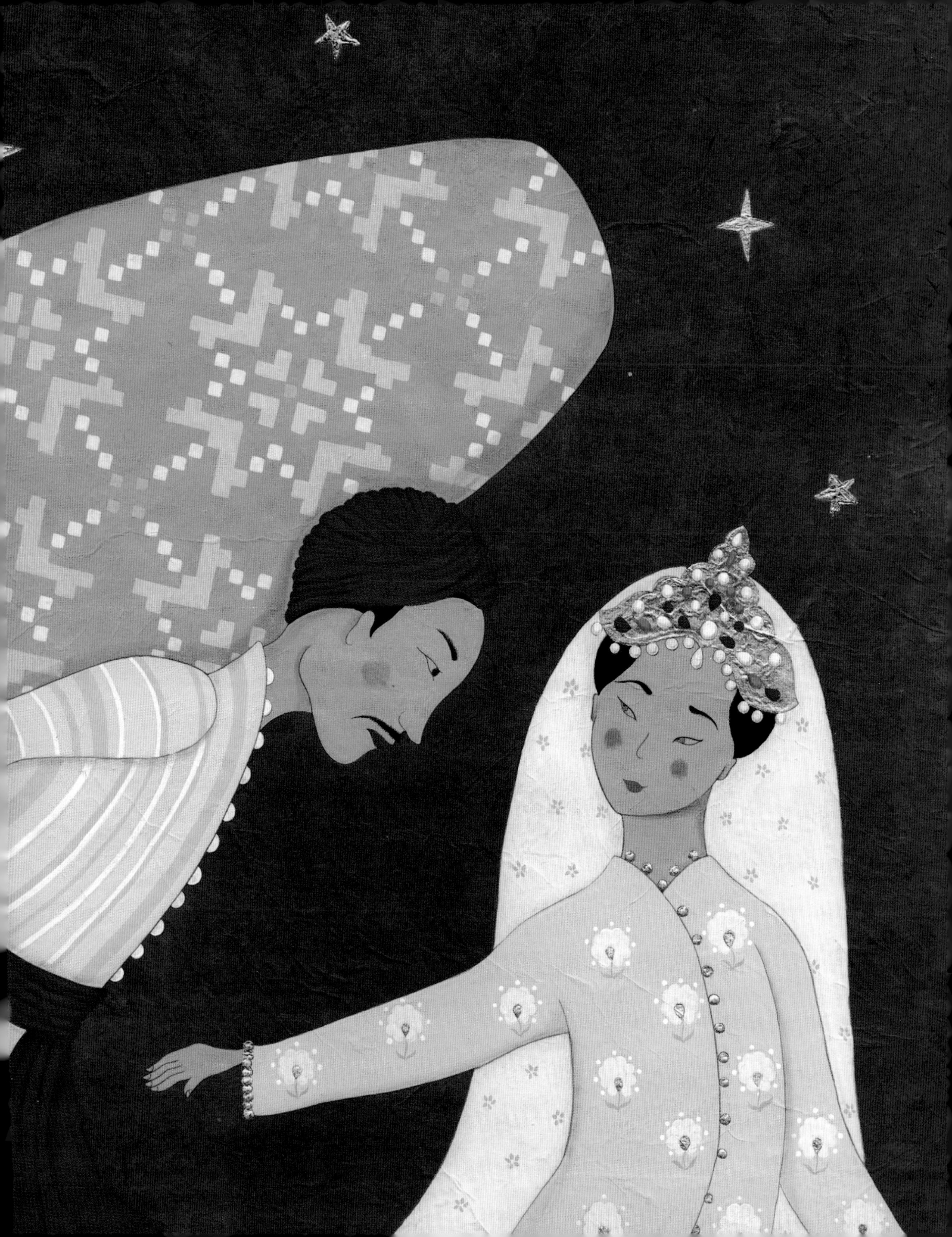

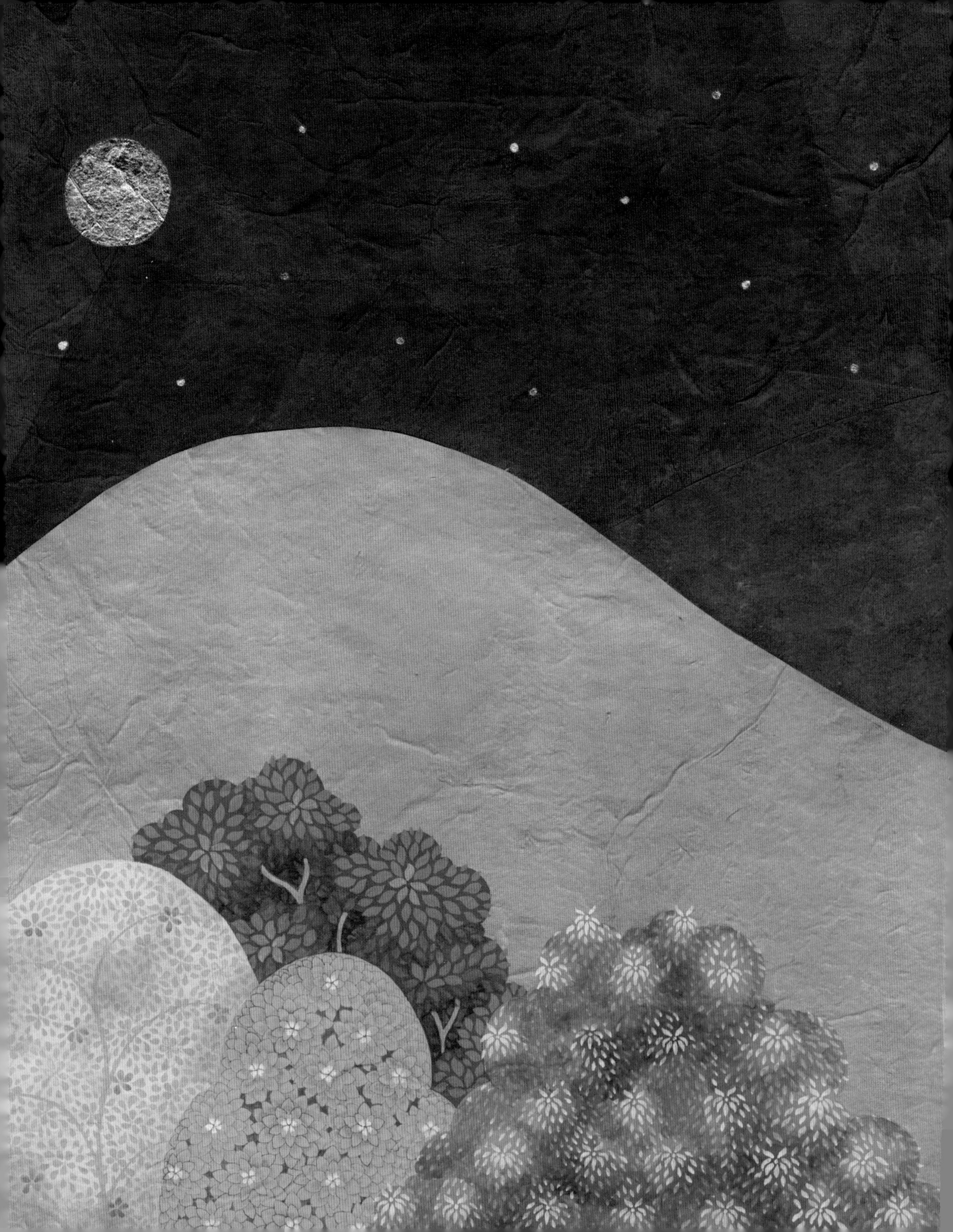

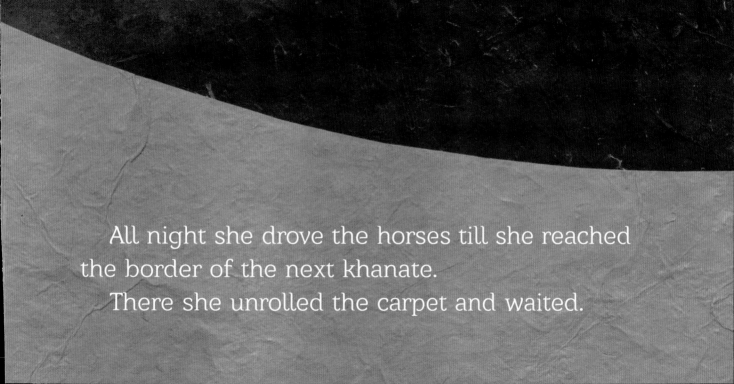

All night she drove the horses till she reached
the border of the next khanate.
There she unrolled the carpet and waited.

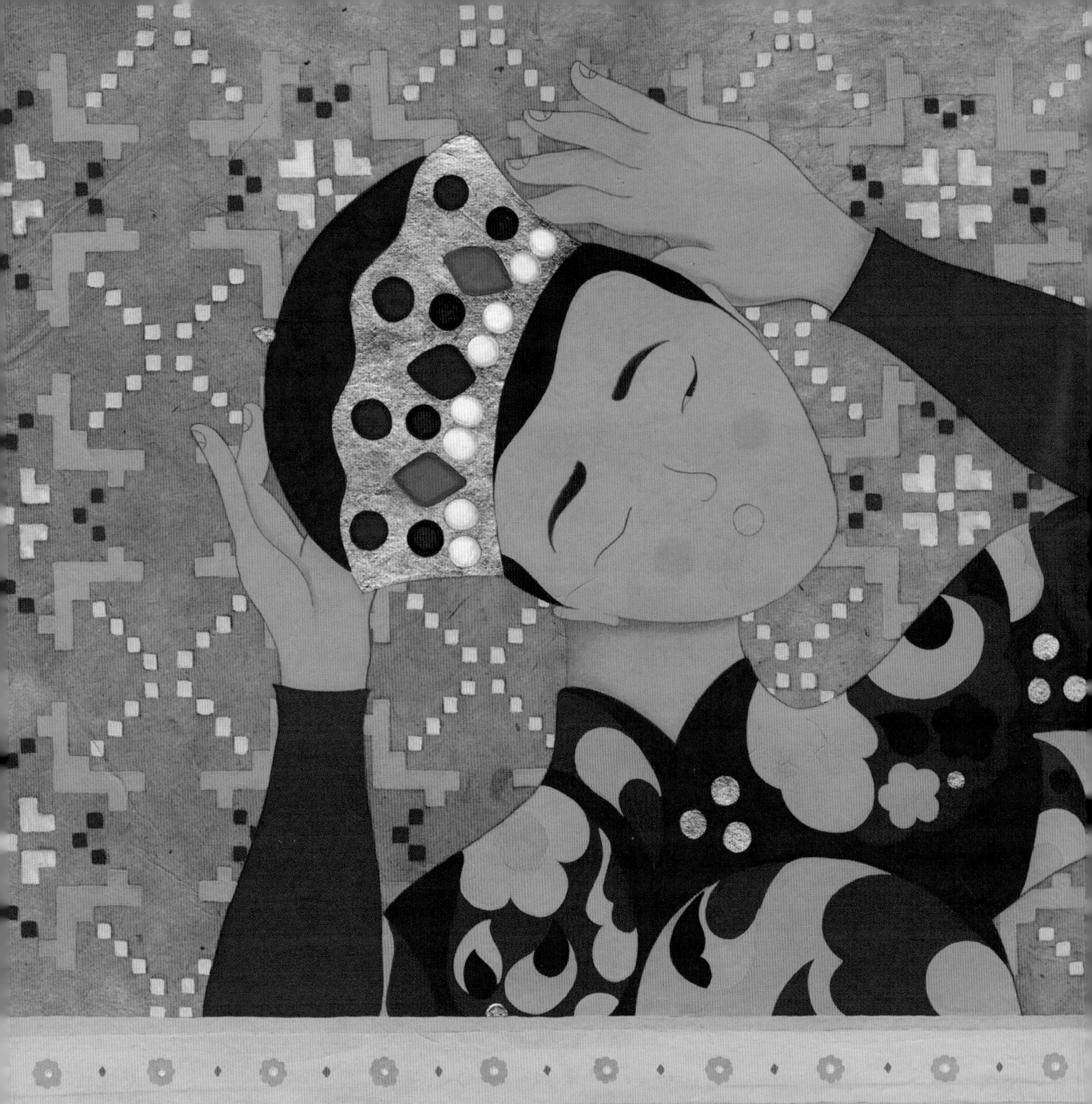

When the sun shone upon Bolotbek's face he sat up and looked around.

"Where am I? What have you done?"

Danyshman said, "I only did what you asked.

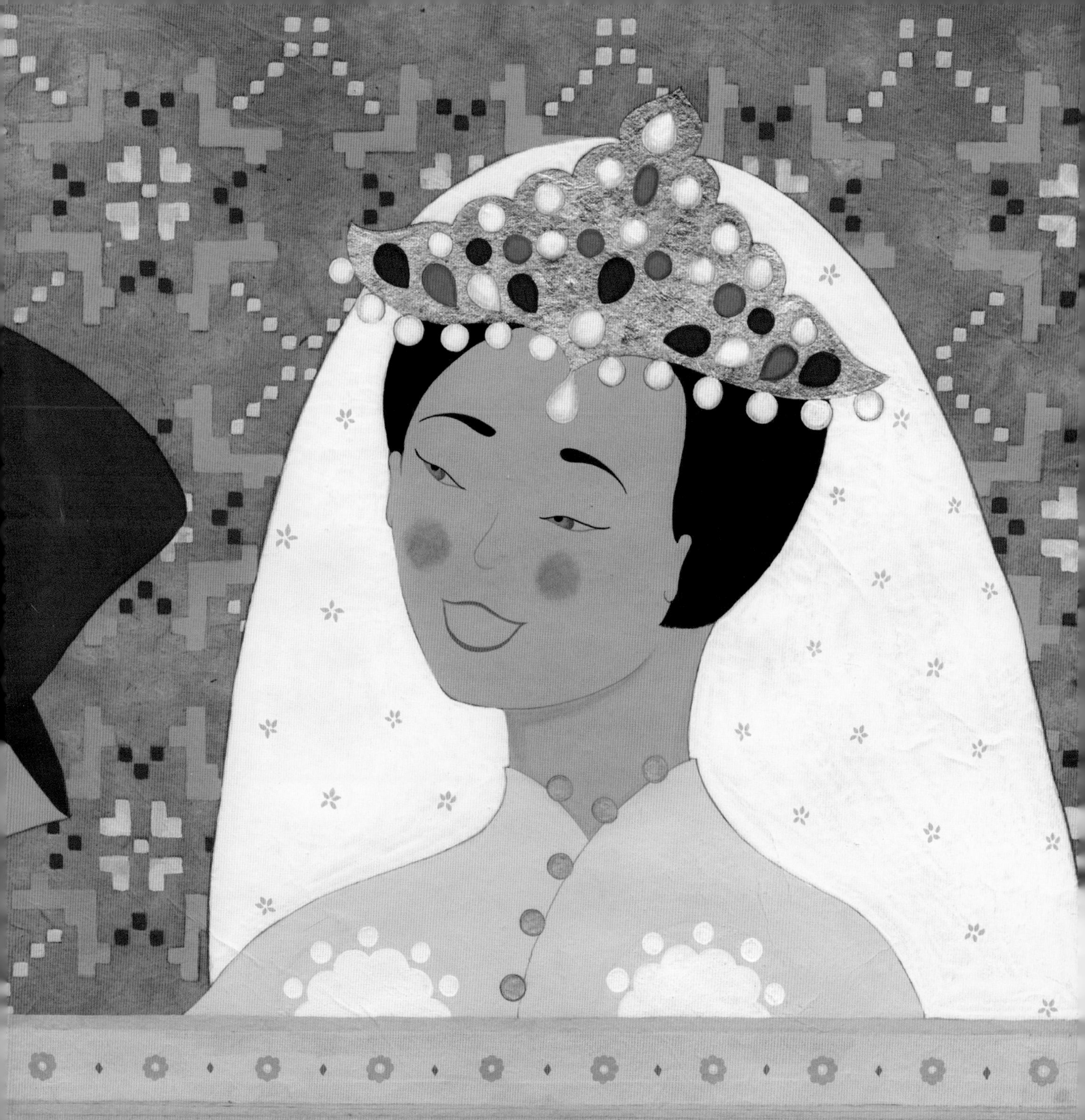

You said to take whatever is most precious and leave your khanate. So I have taken you."

Bolotbek felt silly. Smiling at Danyshman, he said, "Fine, you win. Let's go home."

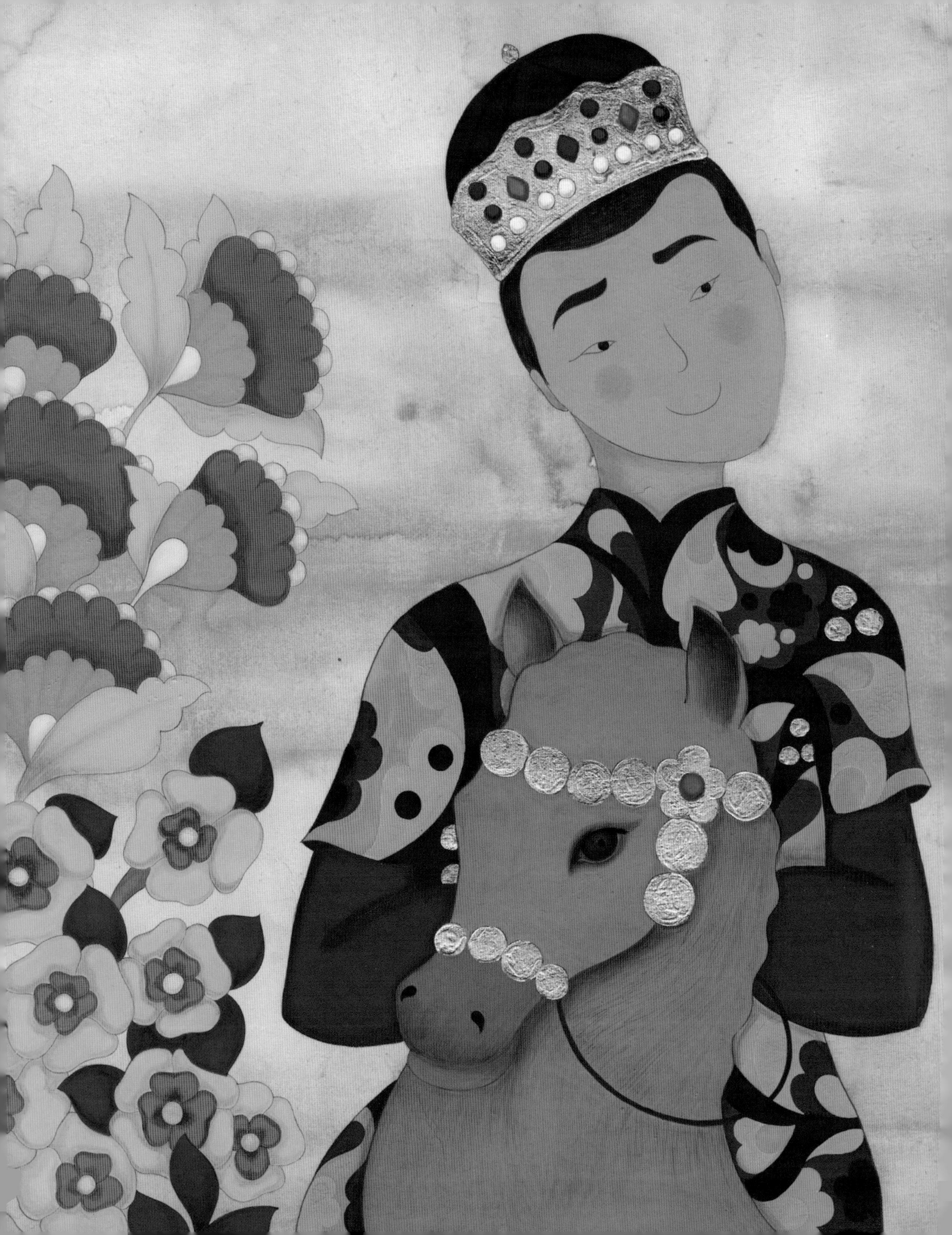

So they returned to their khanate and lived happily ever after.

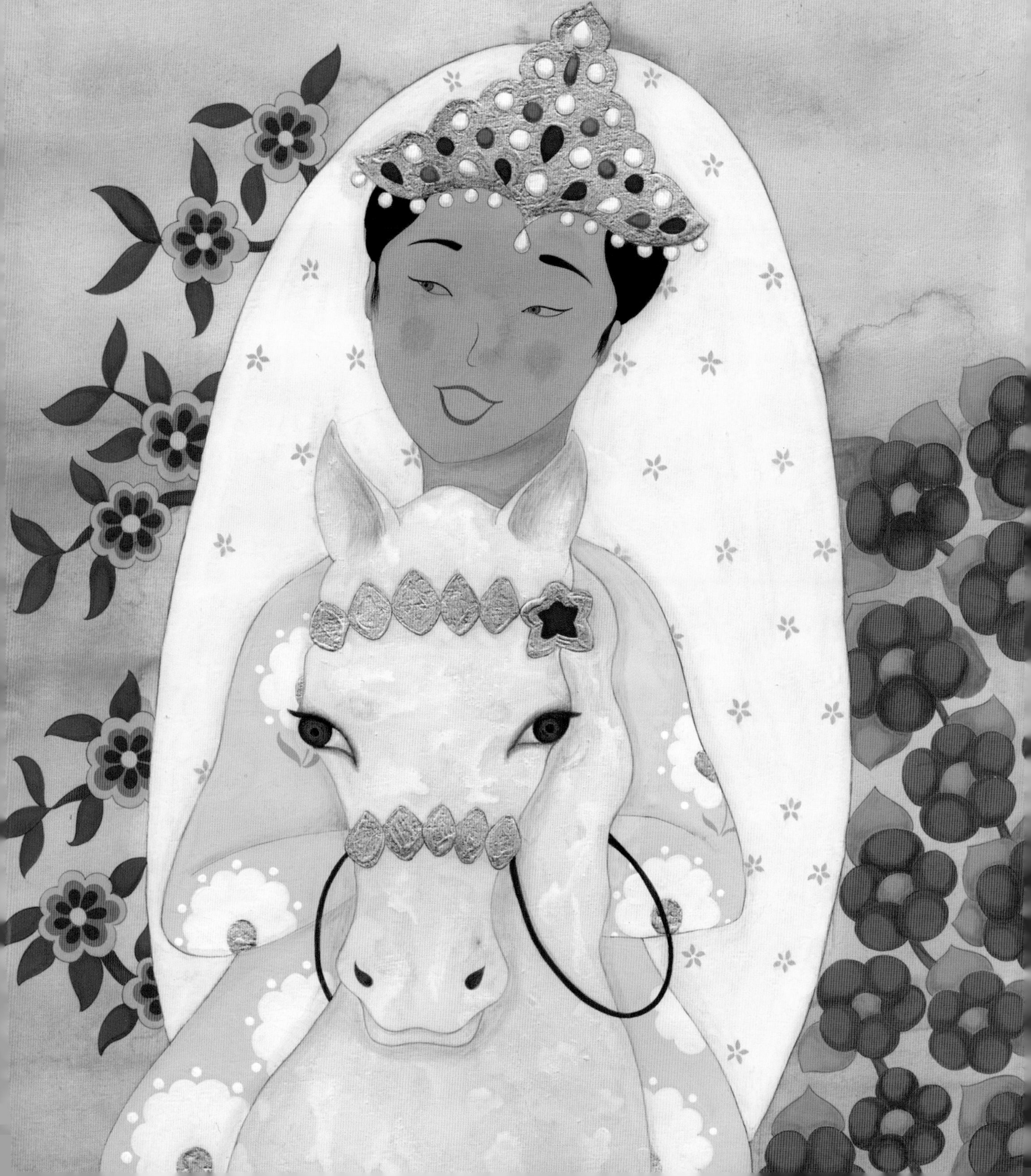